THE OUTLINE OF A HUGE BEAST GLISTENED IN THE SUN . . .

Leah looked up as the monster solidified. Vaguely manlike in shape, its face had no features except for a wide, slavering mouth filled with huge teeth. Four long arms ended in taloned hands. Its strangely smooth gray skin glittered with unnatural luminescence.

As the beast of air and magic bore down upon her, Leah murmured a spell that transformed all her power into a weapon. A long, thin sword of pure energy appeared in her hand. She struck at the beast, but its upper arms blocked her thrust while its lower arms caught her waist in a viselike grip . . .

Today's Best Fantasy from Dell

* denotes an illustrated book

THE SPELLSTONE OF SHALTUS

Linda E. Bushyager

A DELL BOOK

*For the friends whose advice and encouragement
made this book possible—Hank Davis, Gary Far-
ber, Dave Romm, and especially Moshe Feder*

Published by
Dell Publishing Co., Inc.
1 Dag Hammarskjold Plaza
New York, New York 10017

Dell ® TM 681510, Dell Publishing Co., Inc.

ISBN: 0-440-18274-3

Printed in the United States of America

First printing—May 1980

THE SPELLSTONE
OF SHALTUS

One

Something was wrong.

Leah Carlton hesitated on the threshold of Castle Carlton's entryway. While she listened to the lonely hum of crickets behind her, her eyes searched the shadowed hall. It was strangely dark and chill.

Her fingers gripped the doorjamb. Then she stepped forward, letting the door shudder closed behind her.

There was the same wrongness that Leah had felt when she'd left the castle a few days before. But it was stronger now and had taken on a tangible quality that assaulted her physical as well as her psychic senses.

The normally damp air was dank and reeked with the faint odor of rotting vegetation. The air moved too quickly in a cold draft that whistled along the ancient stone walls. Even the torchlight seemed to be affected, as the unnaturally dim flames failed to keep deep shadows from spilling over the floor.

Automatically she used her sorcery to seek the source of the wrongness that now seemed a threat. While her lips soundlessly recited a spell, she spun a probe outward in a thread that wove its way through the castle. The ritual words were almost meaningless, but they helped her channel her thoughts through the powerstone she wore as a necklace. The spellstone focused and enhanced her natural psychic abilities.

At first she felt nothing unusual. Then she sensed a flickering presence. When she tried to explore it, it somehow eluded her magic. For a moment she was aware of an entity, powerful and dangerous, without knowing its form or origin. Then it disappeared, and she could not pick it up again.

Leah blinked and stared at the reality of the murky hallway. It remained shadowed by the wrongness. Although the presence had hidden from her, it still waited within the castle.

There had been something familiar in the menace of that brief touch.

Brushing back a loose strand of her braided, silver hair, she tried to pinpoint the lingering impression of familiarity. Then with a shudder she recognized it—the wraith-being Shaltus.

She shook her head. It could not have been Shaltus; he did not have the power to reach the castle, and, in any case, she would have recognized his touch instantly. Yet the similarity could not be coincidence.

She hurried down the hallway to find her half-brother, Richard S'Carlton. He was a better sorcerer than she was—certainly he must have contacted the presence while she was away.

As she reached the bottom of the main staircase, she hesitated, wondering if she should even mention it to him.

When she'd told him about feeling a wrongness in the castle a week ago, he had scoffed, deriding her psychic talents. She really shouldn't have been surprised or hurt by his reaction, for he found fault with everything she said and did, but it had stung her just the same—enough to make her leave the castle for a few days.

She had gone to her father's old hunting cabin. Increasingly since her father's death two years ago, it had become a haven from the rejection and general hostility at Castle Carlton and from Richard's obvious contempt. Since it lay halfway between the castle and the Sylvan forest of Ayers, it seemed a fittingly ironic place for her retreat, for she was half-Sylvan and half-human, and her mixed parentage was the heart of her human half-brother's hatred and the cause of her ostracism by both worlds.

Still, she knew she would have to speak to Richard, for if the Shaltus-wraith were behind the threat she felt, it could be a danger to him and to her two half-sisters, as well as to herself. Shaltus had killed their father and had vowed to destroy everyone of S'Carlton blood.

Having made up her mind, she moved forward, only to be halted by the sound of a mockingly solicitous voice behind her.

"Lady Leahdes—so you have returned from your trip."

Leah's back stiffened automatically at the greeting, all too aware of the sarcasm in the title the man used. She was not a Lady S'Carlton like her half-sisters, but only a Carlton, and that surname was due to her father's express command, not to any legal tie between him and her mother. Also, the man had used her full name, Leahdes, which was of Sylvan origin, rather than the human-style nickname Leah.

She gritted her teeth and then turned to smile politely down at Frederick Hillard, the chief steward. His eyes glittered with unconcealed enmity.

Hillard had never been friendly, but while her father had been alive he'd at least treated her with a modicum of respect. Now Hillard had more reason than most to hate her, for she was half-Sylvan and his

son had been killed during the recent trouble with
the forest people.

"Yes, I'm back, for a few days anyway. Is my
brother in his rooms?"

"Lord S'Carlton has just gone in to dinner," replied
the steward. "Lord Rowen and his party didn't arrive until late, so dinner was held for them . . ."

"Lord Rowen has arrived?"

Leah felt a mixture of relief and anxiety. When her
half-brother had finally admitted to himself that he
was unable to handle the Shaltus-wraith, he had sent
for Michael Rowen, a sorcerer whose reputation was
exceeded only by the fees he charged for his services. She hoped his reputation was deserved.

"Thank you, Frederick," she said, nodding a dis-
missal. Then she ran upstairs to her room.

Realizing that her presence would be an embar-
rassment to her half-siblings, but determined at least
to see the noted sorcerer and perhaps hear some of
the conversation at the head table, she decided to
slip inconspicuously into the dining hall. Because of
the distinguished guest, the room was bound to be
more noisy and crowded than usual; however, she
knew that she would still have to do something about
her appearance if she didn't want to attract attention.

She slipped out of her riding clothes and put on the
rigid corset and stiff petticoats that human custom
required. She hated the uncomfortable undergarments, but she had to conform. She chose a somber
gown of dark brown wool and heelless slippers to
minimize her height.

Unbinding her two waist-length braids, she lux-
uriated for the moment in the freedom of having
loose hair. However, women in Carlton did not wear
their hair that way. Because she'd been ridiculed
for the things she could not change, she'd learned to
conform to those that she could. So she replaited her

silver hair into a series of thin braids and wrapped
them ornately around her head. Then she clipped on
a brown felt cap that neatly camouflaged most of her
hair.

Finally she turned to the mirror above her dresser
and scrutinized her features, silently cursing the
combination of traits that had made her too human
to be accepted as a Sylvan and yet did not entirely
conceal her Sylvan heredity.

At almost two meters she was too tall for a human
woman; yet the forest people would have considered her short. Her cheekbones were too high, her
lips too full, her skin too pale. Her silver hair was
also unique, but at least it didn't have the greenish
cast of Sylvan hair.

She thought she might have been considered beautiful, in an exotic way, if it hadn't been for her eyes.
They were too large for her face, though not so large
as a Sylvan's, and she had normal pupils. However,
she had inherited the odd-colored eyes of the Sylvan,
and that was probably the most disturbing thing
about her face—one eye was dark brown and one
was turquoise.

Leah quickly applied dark powder to her face.
It made her look less pale and downplayed her
cheekbones, but there was nothing she could do
about her eyes. Still, the drab dress and cap and the
makeup had made a difference, and she looked, if not
quite ordinary, at least inconspicuous.

With a slight slouch that further de-emphasized
her height, she hurried down to dinner.

As she had anticipated, the hall was quite crowded,
so she quietly eased her way over to the tiny table
where she always sat. Tucked between a massive pillar and the entrance to the kitchen, it was unobtrusive but placed her close enough to the raised dais
holding the head table to hear most of what was said,

even though its position against the far left wall didn't give her a very good view.

Although she had not been expected, the table was clear and unoccupied, as though her use of it had contaminated the spot.

Glancing around, Leah noticed that dinner was only half-finished, so she called to one of the serving maids and ordered some wine and the current course. Evidently the larger-than-usual gathering and the overly elaborate meal had slowed the dinner's progress.

The noisy crowded seemed in good spirits; yet Leah sensed a subtle undercurrent of tension. She wondered how many felt the wrongness that still edged her perceptions.

The occupants of the head table seemed especially troubled. They tried to mask their anxiety with a forced gaiety that only underlined the tension.

Leah studied the stranger sitting at the far left seat on the dais, closest to her. From his appearance she guessed that he was one of Lord Rowen's party, but not the sorcerer himself. His dark gray trousers, lighter gray tunic, and black half-cape dangling from his shoulders were sturdy but unadorned. He was about twenty-five or thirty, with close-cropped charcoal-colored hair streaked with premature gray. He was thin, bearded, and rather ordinary looking, except for the fact that he wore spectacles, which was something of an oddity.

To his right sat Richard's garrulous wife, Mary-Esther. She had engaged the man in a one-way conversation that allowed him to do nothing more than nod occasionally. A polite half-smile was pasted to his lips, but every so often it slipped into a worried frown.

Between Mary-Esther and Lord Richard sat Bishop Merion. Leah was rather surprised to see the

N'Omb priest in attendance—he and Richard had not gotten along well since her half-brother had decreased the Church tithe after her father's death.

A few hundred years ago such an act would have been unthinkable—the N'Omb Church had been all-powerful then, controlling almost every aspect of daily life. But with the discovery of spellstones and the subsequent rise of sorcery, the Church's influence had declined. Although the Church first condemned sorcery as it did the forbidden old magic of science, it had been unable to prevent its use. Eventually the Church accepted sorcery's inevitability and began to use for its own purposes. Now the Church sought out spellstones and trained its priests as venerated sorcerers.

Bishop Merion was himself a modest sorcerer. Leah wondered what had made him come to Carlton. Perhaps he was concerned more with ridding the countryside of the Shaltus-wraith than with prolonging the dispute over the tithe. At the moment he was paying more attention to his food than to her half-brother's attempts at conversation.

Evidently the tall, auburn-haired man on Richard's right was Lord Michael Rowen. Leah wished that she could see him better, but her sidewise view showed only his profile, and she was some distance away.

Leah's unmarried half-sister Barbara sat to Lord Rowen's right. When Barbara leaned forward Leah could see that her older sister wore one of her best dresses. Her black hair was pulled up in an elaborate coiffure of curls ornamented with gold and ruby combs, and she wore a matching ruby necklace. She looked quite beautiful. She'd apparently gone to some trouble to impress Lord Rowen, an eligible bachelor.

There was another man to Barbara's right, but Leah couldn't see anything more than his nose bobbing up and down whenever he took a sip of wine, which was often.

When the kitchenmaid brought supper Leah asked the girl for the names of the guests and learned that the fellow with spectacles was Timothy Fletcher and that the man at the far end of the table was called Rusty. The maid knew nothing more about them except that they had both ridden in with Lord Rowen.

As she ate, Leah tried to overhear what was being said at the head table, but the noise from the diners and a group of minstrels lustily singing a ballad drowned the conversation.

She concentrated on her dinner. This course consisted of an apple compote with chopped walnuts, some finely ground bread with blueberry jam, asparagus, and chicken sautéed in wine. Before she had time to do more than taste the chicken, it was replaced by the next course of a heavily spiced venison stew topped with a flaky crust. She decided that it would have taken several days to prepare such a sumptuous feast and that word of Lord Rowen's arrival must have come just after she'd left the castle.

When the minstrels finished their song, one of the people seated near the front of the room rose and bowed to the visiting sorcerer.

"Lord Rowen, we've all looked forward to your arrival very much. I'd like to toast your success in destroying the Shaltus-wraith."

As he lifted his glass, those around him loudly chorused their approval. Many jumped to their feet to drink, while others in the back of the room stamped and pounded their tables in jovial agreement. Although they were suspicious of sorcery, they were realistic enough to favor its use against an enemy. And since the ruling S'Carltons were sorcerers, they'd been forced to accept its use in everyday life.

Lord Rowen stood and nodded his thanks, but the

grim line of his mouth made Leah think that he had some doubt as to his ability to defeat the wraith. She wondered just how much Rowen would be able to accomplish. No one knew the full extent of Shaltus's power, only that it was malevolent and deadly.

Leah's throat tightened as she thought of her father. He had fought Shaltus.

At first he hadn't recognized the nature of the strange blighted area in the Blue River Valley that had appeared at the end of the S'Shegan War. Trees began to grow at odd angles on farms with stunted crops; terrified farmers whispered stories of deformed calves and disappearing livestock. Then men vanished.

Her father tried to destroy the wraith, but its defenses were too strong. Gradually the evil hole grew into a twenty-square-kilometer blight of destruction that threatened Castle Bluefield in southern Carlton, and Lord S'Carlton's sorcery could only slow its growth. A little over two years ago he had finally engaged the wraith in an all-out duel.

Lord S'Carlton had died, and Castle Bluefield had been taken over by the strange Shaltus force.

Although Richard had taken his father's place as Lord of the kingdom of Carlton, he'd been unable to match his father's necromantic ability. So the area affected had increased even faster than before. Death or madness touched any nonsorcerer entering the region, and so far no sorcerer had been able to get closer than a kilometer to the Shaltus spellstone at its heart.

Leah studied Lord Rowen, who remained standing in acknowledgment of yet another toast. He was a very large man, tall and massively built, yet not overweight.

With his thick shoulders, long arms, and oversized hands, he looked quite powerful, but his finely chiseled features and confident bearing gave an overall impression of intelligence rather than brawn. He was clean shaven, and his reddish-brown hair was almost shoulder length. He was younger than she'd expected, perhaps in his early thirties.

The sorcerer wore a forest green velvet tunic embroidered with silver and gold over a silver-colored shirt and dark trousers. The matching green and silver half-cape was trimmed with verdant green osmur fur. A dark brown belt with a large silver buckle and a sheath knife circled his waist. The fineness of the materials and workmanship were a testament to Rowen's success as a sorcerer.

Around his neck hung a sizable amethyst-colored crystal. It was a powerstone, and like the smaller gem in the necklace Leah wore, it could amplify the psychic powers of its owner. A certain amount of psychic ability was necessary to use the spellstones, whose power was dependent on the person's natural capabilities and on the length of time the person used the stone. Since no one was quite certain how the stones worked, they were controlled chiefly by the recitation of ritualized spells that helped focus the user's thoughts through the stone.

Different superstitions and myths tried to explain the power of the stones. Some sorcerers believed the spellstones drew energy from the sun and moon, and they devised elaborate rites to try to pull more power from these sources. But Leah doubted either really powered the stones, for they worked just as well on cloudy days as on clear ones. Her father had speculated that the stones linked the earth to another dimension and drew energy from there. And the N'Omb Church doctrine said that N'Omb himself supplied the power, which was why the stones had been found only in certain taboo areas consecrated to N'Omb.

While some sorcerers feared their spellstones almost as much as the commoners did, Leah accepted hers as she accepted her hands and used it as naturally.

Suddenly Rowen turned toward Leah as though he had felt her stare. Self-consciously she shrank back against the pillar, out of his line of sight. However, the sorcerer continued to gaze curiously in her direction. Then the start of a toast addressed to Lord S'Carlton distracted his attention. Rowen sat down as Richard stood.

Leah's half-brother was also an imposing figure, but he was not quite so tall as Lord Rowen nor so heavily built. The long-sleeved red brocade tunic he wore emphasized his broad shoulders and slim waist. Like Barbara, Richard had lustrous jet black hair and deepset brown eyes. His hair just touched his collar. His beard was short and neatly trimmed.

Smiling at the assembly, he answered the toast to his health with one of his own. His deep voice cut through the noisy room like a knife: "To Lord Rowen's success and to our kingdom's prosperity."

As Leah raised her glass in response, she suddenly gasped. The glass slipped from her fingers, rolled across the table, and spilled wine that stained the tablecloth blood red.

In that instant the feeling of wrongness welled up and smashed against her like an icy wave. The dark presence she had felt earlier flooded her senses. Now its Shaltus origin was unmistakable. Yet it remained strangely different from the Shaltus-wraith itself.

Instinctively focusing her powers through her spellstone to protect herself, she realized that she was feeling only the blacklash of the attack. Her half-brother was its target.

On the dais, Richard had jerked backward as though he had been struck by a physical blow. The powerstones in his wristlet blazed blue-white in protective response.

The backlash also hit Barbara. She began to scream.

A freezing wind rushed through the hall. It snuffed out candles and lanterns, plunging the room into dark chaos.

Leah shuddered as the backlash of force continued to pound her. Struggling to overcome the paralyzing fear, she pulled out her spellstone and concentrated on it. It reacted sluggishly, finally glowing faintly in response. She sensed that her half-brother was under fierce attack. Instinctively she cast counterspells to aid him, but they seemed to have no effect.

Pushing past frightened diners trying to escape the room, she headed toward the main table. As she reached the edge of the dais, shadows seemed to pile on shadows around her. She took another step and found herself in an unnatural black maelstrom of magic. Her spellstone was a pinpoint of light.

When she tried to move she felt as though she were struggling through quicksand that pressed against her face and chest, suffocating her. Gasping, she forced herself forward, using all of her strength to fight the formless evil surrounding her. The room was strangely silent, as though the force blotted out sound as well as light.

Then she saw the glow of another spellstone in the darkness. She stumbled against the edge of the platform, grabbed hold of one of the legs of the head table, and pulled herself onto the dais.

As she tripped over an upturned chair, a large hand caught her and pulled her upright. The hand grasped hers in a powerful grip. A spellstone centimeters away blazed blue-white.

Lips pressed against her ear and shouted words that the Shaltus-force muffled into a whisper. Making out enough to recognize the spell, Leah began to recite it along with him. As she did so the voice grew louder, and her own stone grew brighter until it matched the color and intensity of the other's stone. She felt a flow of power that pushed back the darkness.

Then she recognized the man who gripped her hand so tightly. It was Lord Rowen.

A feeling of urgency stronger than her fear swept over her. She had to reach her half-brother.

When she tried to free her fingers from Rowen's grasp, he realized her intention. As she moved forward he followed, still tightly holding onto her hand.

The center of the disturbance was a black vortex that encircled her half-brother.

Leah touched the swirling shadows. Her fingers met a rock-hard wall of force. She could sense her half-brother weakening. He would not be able to withstand the Shaltus-force much longer on his own.

Instinctively she pushed against the barrier with her will. She could not move forward. But the tall sorcerer stepped through.

Leah remained pressed to the shadow-wall. Her arm extended half-way into it, still clutching Rowen's left hand. She wondered how he'd overcome the magic.

The sorcerer reached into the swirling blackness with his other arm and grabbed Richard. Instantly the three of them were linked together. The evil vortex expanded around them.

The flow of energy increased. The focus was Richard, backed with Rowen's and Leah's strength. As the energy flowed through them to Richard, he used it to fight the Shaltus-force.

For a moment that seemed an eternity Leah felt her strength drain, until she thought she had no more to give. But the pressure of Michael Rowen's hand on hers seemed to demand more from her, and somehow she continued to channel power to him.

Suddenly the darkness of an unlighted, enclosed

room replaced the unnatural blackness. The suppressed sounds returned in a cacophony of confusion. Leah discovered that she was shouting a power spell in unison with her half-brother and Rowen. With the cessation of the attack their voices broke off abruptly.

Rowen released Leah's hand. She raised it to her lips and sucked on the bloody gouges his fingernails had cut. Her own nails had made similar marks on his palm.

Rowen muttered a spell that rekindled the extinguished candles in the hall's great chandeliers. It took Leah's eyes a moment to readjust to light that revealed the wreckage of overturned tables and chairs, spilled food and broken dishes, smashed glasses, and torn hangings.

Most of the diners and servants were still inside the room. With the return of light they huddled together in confusion. Although they had not been the target of the attack, the use of sorcery terrified them. They did not understand it, they had no defense against it, and they had a superstitious dread of it that magnified their fear.

Suddenly Leah felt faint. As she swayed, Rowen slid his arm around her waist, and she felt a short surge of strength flow into her.

A look of mild surprise crossed his face as he noticed her mismatched eyes—one deep brown, one startling turquoise. She saw the look and tried to pull away, also realizing that her cap had been dislodged during the confusion. Her braids were as silver as moonlight. But Rowen took her hand gently, yet firmly, in his and would not let it go.

"So, you must be Lord S'Carlton's infamous sister." His deep gray eyes were warm and friendly. "I thought I'd caught a glimpse of you just before this fracas started. Lady Leahdes, isn't it?"

She winced at the title and pulled her hand from his grasp, although she sensed that he did not realize the insult.

"Just Leah."

Then she pushed her way past the sorcerer to her half-brother. A trickle of blood ran from the corner of his mouth. He looked pale and exhausted.

"Richard, are you all right?"

His eyes focused on her face. He nodded and then grimaced as he realized that she had been the one helping Lord Rowen. Brusquely turning away from her, he searched the platform for Barbara.

Even though she could have expected no other reaction from Richard, Leah flinched. She wondered if she could ever become indifferent to his hatred. Forcing her face into an impassive mask, she followed Richard's gaze.

Barbara lay under an overturned section of the head table. Before Leah could move to aid her half-sister, Michael Rowen touched her arm and gestured that she remain where she was. Then he strode over to the injured girl.

Barbara had not inherited much of her father's psychic talents, and she had no spellstone. Thus she had been able to do little to protect herself from the attack. But she was just sensitive enough to be susceptible to its backlash.

While Richard and Michael Rowen tried to rouse Barbara, Leah turned her attention to the others who had been seated at the head table. Richard's wife, Mary-Esther, was hysterical but apparently unhurt. She was being comforted by Bishop Merion. He'd evidently been able to protect himself from the side effects of the attack on Richard.

The bespectacled Timothy Fletcher had tripped and fallen off the platform in the darkness. He sat on the floor nursing a bruised head.

Rusty, a stocky man of about fifty, was still seated in his chair at the now overturned table. From the redness of his cheeks, nose, and eyes, he'd apparently been enjoying the wine quite a bit during the dinner. Yet his thoughtful, worried expression indicated that the events of the past few minutes had sobered him.

He noticed Leah's appraisal and stared back. His pale blue eyes revealed a keen intelligence that his oafish appearance belied. He sauntered over to her, glancing calmly around the room as though unsurprised by the turn of events.

"Don't you think you'd better make some explanation to these people, miss?" he asked Leah.

"Me?" She looked nervously at the frightened knots of servants, castle guardsmen, townspeople, and other guests still clustered in the hall. She possessed neither their allegiance nor their respect.

Knowing that something would have to be said, she crossed to her half-brother, who still knelt at Barbara's side.

Leah touched his shoulder. "Lord Rowen and I will get her to her room. You'd better take charge here."

Richard glanced around with a frown.

Michael Rowen nodded agreement. "I think she'll be all right. The thing that attacked you will have to rest for a few hours, perhaps a few days, before it regains enough energy to strike again. We'll have to use that time to rest and to organize a proper defense."

"What was it? It was like Shaltus; yet it was not like him. But it couldn't have been the Shaltus-wraith—nothing has the power to reach so far. . . ." Richard shook his head wearily.

"I'm certain Shaltus controlled it," interjected Leah. "If he can attack us at this distance . . ." As she spoke and realized the implication of the attack, her stomach knotted in fear. The normal range for sorcery was only about five to eight kilometers. The Shaltus spellstone lay some hundred and thirty kilometers to the south.

"No," said Lord Rowen decisively. "It was not Shaltus. Not even a wraith has that kind of power. The source of the attack was something inside the castle. It was sent and shaped by Shaltus, but it wasn't Shaltus himself. And it's still here."

"But what was it?" asked Richard as he rose to his feet.

"A powerstone programmed by Shaltus and planted here by someone under his control." Rowen shook his head. "I'll have to study this situation before I can tell you more."

He gestured at his friend. "Rusty, give me a hand with this girl." As the two men lifted Barbara, the sorcerer asked Leah to show them to her half-sister's room.

Leading the way past the still stunned dinner guests, Leah felt the beginnings of the sense of wrongness return. It was greatly diminished, but it was still there. She knew that Lord Rowen had been right— the Shaltus-controlled presence lay hidden within the castle, and it would attack again—soon.

Two

"Will she be all right?" asked Leah. She was alarmed by her half-sister's ashen stillness. Barbara had been only a little kinder to her than Richard since their father's death, but she was still her sister.

Although Michael Rowen bent over Barbara, using his spellstone to probe her injuries, it was Rusty who replied.

"Aye, she'll come out of it, miss."

Surprised by the certainty in his craggy voice, Leah turned to stare at the man. Although his eyes were red-veined and watery from a lifetime of too much alcohol, there was an intensity about them that told of knowledge, wisdom, and pain. They seemed to have seen too much and known too much.

"You sound sure of it," she said, studying his face.

"I am." His quiet answer seemed no empty reassurance, but rather an undeniable statement of fact.

"Lady Leahdes, I need your help."

Leah's cheeks flushed in anger as she whirled to face Rowen. Then she realized that he didn't mean anything by the title. He was only trying to be polite.

"I told you before, I'm just called Leah. I'm a Carlton, not a S'Carlton, I'm a . . ." The word "half-breed" stuck in her throat. Her mind replaced it in quick succession with the other names she'd been called—bastard, Sylvie, mongrel, tree-eater, illegitimate; and as the Sylvan labeled her with more politeness but equal rejection—a *shiffem*—their term for a female child of half-Sylvan blood.

She forced back the words and said calmly, "I'm a commoner—not a lady."

Michael Rowen looked embarrassed.

"That's all right," Leah continued with a note of forgiveness in her voice that she did not really feel. "It's a natural mistake. Now, what can I do to help you?"

"Put your spellstone on top of mine," he said. His powerstone rested on Barbara's forehead. "Then put your hands over mine and link with me."

"Isn't that dangerous?" She'd always been taught not to let her stone come into contact with any other powerstone.

"Not with proper control."

She hesitated, then knelt by his side, removed her necklace, and placed her stone on top of his. She tensed as the surfaces of the two crystals touched. She felt no adverse reaction, however, only a slight tingling on the edges of her awareness.

Rowen cupped his hands over the stones, which began to glow with a warm white light.

Again Leah hesitated, still wondering whether Rowen knew what he was doing. There was something about the friendliness in his dove gray eyes that made her trust him. She placed her hands over his.

Concentrating on her stone, she found herself linked to Rowen as she had been before. He whispered a healing spell, and she recited it with him.

The ritual words helped her focus on the crystal and channel her power through it. Her psychic awareness increased and altered. The chant became a steady, rhythmic beat. She was hardly aware of it or of her surroundings anymore.

She could feel Barbara's presence now, a faint throb of life like a tiny pool of water at the bottom of a deep well. She seemed to be following Rowen down that well. Her hands pressed tightly against his.

At the bottom the well became a swirling tunnel of fog and then a dense black vortex, similar to that which had surrounded Richard. It grew harder to move. She felt strangely weak.

They were very close to Barbara now. They pushed against the darkness inside her mind, forcing it away, trying to free her from it. They touched her and held her. With all their will they pulled her upward, feeding energy back into her, forcing her out of the well of darkness.

Without warning Leah's strength failed. Her link to Rowen dissolved. She spun away, back down into the dark well. For an awful moment she was alone, without the slightest bit of energy left to fight. The darkness seemed suddenly vast, peaceful, and irresistible.

Then the contact between her mind and Barbara's snapped. Leah opened her eyes to find that Rowen had grabbed the stones from Barbara's forehead and now held them clenched together in white-knuckled hands several centimeters above Barbara's face.

Leah pulled her hands back from his and rubbed them together. They were like ice.

She felt lightheaded.

Rowen slipped her talisman around her neck, took her hands in his, and studied her with concern.

"I'm sorry—I didn't realize that you were still so weak from our bout with the Shaltus-stone. Sorcery takes far more energy than we sometimes realize. If we expend too much, it can be dangerous. When I felt you lose control I had to break contact."

"Barbara?" said Leah anxiously. When she looked down at her half-sister she saw that the girl's face looked pinker and healthier. She was now breathing more easily.

"It looks as though we did some good after all," said Rowen.

Barbara stirred. Her eyes blinked, opened, and slowly focused on his face.

"How are you feeling?" asked Rowen. He took Barbara's hand in his. It seemed twice as large as hers.

"I . . . just very tired . . . what . . ."

"Relax, you just need some sleep now." He glanced at Leah. "So do we." Then he turned back to Barbara and gently smoothed her hair. As he began to tell her what had happened, her eyes closed.

"She's all right now," said Rusty. "She's fallen asleep."

Michael Rowen patted Barbara's head once more. Then he rubbed his chin thoughtfully. Turning back to Leah he said, "You know, I believe the spellstone was planted here specifically to attack those of you with S'Carlton blood. From what your brother has told me about Shaltus it seems that the wraith's main goal is to destroy your family in retaliation for what your father did to him. The stone is here just to strike those of S'Carlton blood—that's why you and Barbara were the ones mainly affected by the backlash from the attack on Richard."

"Bishop Merion and the others seemed unharmed," added Leah.

Suddenly she realized that there were others of S'Carlton blood within the castle—her nephews, Richard's two little boys. What if they had been hurt by the blacklash . . .

Wordlessly she was on her feet, running for the door —but a terrible weakness washed over her before she'd taken a half-dozen steps. She fell.

Somehow Rusty had gotten there in front of her, as though he'd known in advance of her sudden dash across the room. He caught her as she collapsed.

She blacked out for a few seconds. When she came

to she found both Rusty and Lord Rowen bending over her. Dizzily she tried to bring their faces into focus.

"Now where did you think you were going?" asked Rusty, running his fingers repeatedly through his graying, reddish hair in agitation.

"The children . . . Richard's . . . his boys could have been hurt in the attack."

Michael Rowen's face spun before her eyes. "It's all right. They are out of the castle. I sent them away when I arrived."

"Away?" She shut her eyes against the spinning room.

"They're up in the kingdom of Richmond visiting your other sister and her husband." Leah's eldest half-sister, Laurie, had married the Lord of Richmond, one of the states that along with Carlton made up the loose alliance known as the Eastern Kingdoms.

"They'll be safe there," continued Rowen. "When we got here Rusty felt that something was about to happen and suggested that we get them out of the castle. I guess we should have sent Barbara too . . ."

He squeezed Leah's hand, and she felt a short burst of energy that steadied the world around her. Realizing that Rowen was draining his own reserves of energy to help her, she pulled her hand away.

"Do you think you can walk now, miss?" asked Rusty.

Leah nodded, and they helped her stand. She felt totally exhausted.

"You've got to get some food and then some rest," said Lord Rowen. "And so do I. Rusty, will you please see if you can get something for us to eat."

He led Leah into Barbara's sitting room and made her lie down on the couch. Then with a sigh he collapsed into one of the overstuffed armchairs.

Leah's head swam with questions, but when she

closed her eyes she couldn't summon enough energy to open them again or even to form her chaotic thoughts into any order. Images spun across the backs of her eyelids in a kaleidoscope of color that seemed to draw her farther and farther into its center . . .

Then the sound of soft voices intruded into incoherent dreams. Leah yawned and opened her eyes. Rusty had returned with his friend Tim Fletcher. Groggily she realized that she had fallen asleep.

Michael Rowen had also dozed off. He sprawled in his chair like an oversized stuffed toy bear, his long arms drooping over the sides and his legs propped up on a hassock.

The other two men sat across the room talking quietly. Evidently they'd decided to let Rowen and Leah rest.

"Why is this Shaltus-wraith after the S'Carlton family anyway?" Rusty was saying. Yawning again, Leah closed her eyes and sleepily listened to them.

Fletcher frowned. "Well, it all goes back to its origins, I suppose. You know how a wraith is formed?"

Rusty poured himself another glass of brandy. "A little . . ."

"When a sorcerer dies sometimes he can transfer his, well, soul, if you want to call it that, into his spellstone."

"His memories?" asked the other.

"Some, but not all, I suspect. Mostly it's his will, his spirit." Fletcher helped himself to a sandwich from the cartload of food that Rusty had brought. "Of course such a transfer requires time and preparation, so it can't be done if a sorcerer dies suddenly. In Shaltus's case, he had the time, will, and reason. From what I know, it happened during the last days of the Great War between the Eastern Kingdoms and S'Shegan. Shaltus was one of S'Shegan's lieutenants. He was directing the invasion of Carlton and Westvirn.

During the fighting he captured Castle Bluefield and Richard S'Carlton's wife. Shaltus raped and then killed her."

Rusty's head jerked up from his glass. "This Richard?"

Fletcher shook his head. "No—Richard, senior—the present Lord's father. Anyway, S'Carlton, senior, later managed to retake his castle and capture Shaltus. In retaliation for what Shaltus had done to his wife S'Carlton tortured Shaltus and then hung him from the castle wall in a body-fitting cage as a public spectacle until the clothes and flesh rotted from his bones—a slow, hideous death.

Leah's eyes blinked open. Although she had heard the story often, its repetition still evoked gruesome images.

"But Shaltus was a sorcerer," said Rusty. "How could he remain caged, waiting to die?"

Sitting up, Leah answered the question before Fletcher could speak. "It was a cage of silver mesh, impervious to sorcery."

"Oh, we didn't mean to wake you, miss," said Rusty, rising slowly to his feet. His fat cheeks had a rosy flush from the alcohol. "As long as you're awake though, you'd better have something to eat and drink."

While the ruddy-faced man poured Leah a glass of brandy, Fletcher brought her a plate of sandwiches and cold chicken.

"We haven't been introduced—I'm a friend of Lord Rowen's, one Timothy Fletcher—scribbler, scholar, swordsman, and your humble servant, Miss Carlton." With that introduction he bowed his head formally, took her hand, kissed it lightly, and handed her the plate of food.

"Thank you." She wondered if he was being facetious. She wasn't used to such courtesy. Noticing the plate he'd given her, she realized that she felt ravenously hungry. She grabbed a sandwich and began to wolf it down.

"Was I asleep long?" she asked between bites.

Rusty handed her a glass of brandy. "Not long, maybe an hour, an hour and a half—it took me some time to extricate this food from the confusion in the dining room."

Sipping the liquor gratefully, Leah realized that the source of her hunger was the expenditure of so much energy during the sorcery. She would have to be careful. Sorcery was fatiguing at best. Prolonged over-use of psychic powers could result in their loss, even in death. If Shaltus were to attack again, before she could replace the energy, she would be in trouble.

As she thought about it, her fingers stroked her spellstone absentmindedly. She made a swift probe of the castle. The Shaltus-presence remained weak.

"Now, Tim," said Rusty, refilling his glass, "I know silver blocks sorcery and unamplified psychic talents like telepathy and precognition, which don't require spellstones, but if Shaltus died in a silver cage, how did he become a wraith? They're bound by silver as well, aren't they?"

Fletcher nodded. "As I understand it, Shaltus was wearing a large spellstone when he was imprisoned. Realizing that he was dying and unable to escape, he followed the necessary procedures to imprint the stone with his personality. When he died he became a wraith.

"I doubt Lord S'Carlton even knew about wraiths then—I've heard that the technique for making them was discovered by S'Shegan and passed on to some of his sorcerers. That's why the Great War produced so few wraiths, and those were only from S'Shegan's side. I know of none formed before the war. Still, S'Carlton was a careful man, and he knew enough not to bury Shaltus's remains without protection. So the whole cage—powerstone, bones, and all—was taken from the castle and buried some distance away.

"Unfortunately S'Carlton hadn't reckoned with grave robbers. The silver cage was valuable, and powerstones are rare, very rare, so even one tainted by a man as evil as Shaltus was still worth a great deal. However, the thieves found a deadly treasure. When they opened the cage to get the stone they freed the wraith and became its first victims.

"Somehow during his agonized death Shaltus imprinted his desire for revenge on his spellstone. His wraith is not going to be satisfied until its destroys the entire S'Carlton family."

As he finished the story Fletcher sank back down on one of the chairs in the corner of the room and propped up his feet on a low table.

Rusty smiled sardonically. "Well, the wraith may be especially keen on killing off the S'Carltons, but I don't think it would mind it a bit if it managed to destroy the rest of us as well."

His pale blue eyes took on a faraway look that became an intense stare into space, as though he'd gone into a trance. Beads of sweat glistened on his forehead. His shoulders slumped forward. His brow furled, his teeth clenched, and his lips twisted into a grimace.

Suddenly his eyes refocused on reality, and the pained expression slipped from his face. He grabbed his glass violently, took a long swallow that drained it, and refilled it.

"Not enough to drink," he muttered. He took another gulp. His face had turned a shade redder. He swayed slightly. Leah wondered if he were going to pass out.

Then he glanced at her. "You'd better get some real sleep, miss. The next attack won't be for hours yet—not till well after dawn." His words had become slurred.

"How do you . . . you're a precog!" exclaimed Leah, as the bits and pieces came together.

She had never met one before, but she'd heard stories about precogs. There were several precognitive N'Omb oracles. She'd also heard of clairvoyants who lived so much in the future that they went insane. She wondered what it would be like to foresee the future—and she began to speculate on the reasons for Rusty's drinking.

There was pain in the man's too-wise eyes. "Aye."

"What's going to happen?"

"I don't rightly know." He raised his glass in a toastlike gesture, and his hand shook. "My friend here blocks most of it. Michael's going to search for the hidden stone, and he'll find it all right . . ." His words blurred together more, and Fletcher rose to put a steadying hand on the man's arm. "But that's when the thing will attack."

"And then?" asked Fletcher. He took the glass from the other's shaking fingers.

"Don't know. . . ." Rusty blinked once, closed his eyes, and suddenly collapsed like a rag doll.

Tim Fletcher seemed to have been expecting it and caught him firmly with his right hand, hardly spilling the drink in his left. He gently lowered his friend into one of the chairs.

"What now?" asked Leah. She put down her empty plate of food.

"To know the future and to act on it is to change it," replied Fletcher. "Maybe Rusty will be able to tell us when the alcohol wears off a bit. He tries to saturate himself with the stuff to stop his precognition, but he's never entirely successful. In the morning he'll be sober for a short while; perhaps he'll be able to tell us where the Shaltus-controlled stone is hidden. In the meantime you'd better do as he advised and get some more sleep."

Leah rose, looking uncertainly at Barbara's bedroom door and at Rowen's sleeping figure.

Fletcher smiled reassuringly. "Don't worry about them. I'll wake Michael if your sister's condition changes. I'd rather not disturb him now. Go on."

She nodded and headed for her room.

While her father lived, she'd had a suite of rooms all to herself near his. Now she had only a tiny chamber just down the hall from the servants' quarters.

She had been her father's favorite child, despite her illegitimacy. She believed he had loved her Sylan mother deeply. When her mother had died in childbirth, he'd taken Leah in as though she were one of his legitimate children.

Leah thought that in his own mind he'd considered himself married to her mother, even though he'd had a wife. She knew he'd been forced into marriage to seal an alliance with Carlton's neighboring kingdom of Westvirn. Yet she wondered why he had fallen in love with a Sylvan woman. Even in those days there had been hatred between the Sylvan and the humans. Her mother had been the daughter of the chief of the Ayers tribe. His relationship with her helped cement better relations between the humans and the Sylvan.

When her father died, the fragile peace began to crumble. Although there had not yet been a war, it seemed inevitable. Already there had been border clashes and raids by both sides.

Once inside her room Leah unbound her long, silver hair and brushed it out, changed into a light cotton nightgown, and climbed into bed.

She felt exhausted and uneasy. The Shaltus presence seemed stronger now. She focused on her spellstone and again probed the castle, but she could not determine the whereabouts of the Shaltus-programmed stone.

Hoping that Rusty's prediction about the time of the next attack was correct, she forced her tense body to relax. She had to rest. Gradually her body's fatigue prevailed over her anxiety, and she fell into a troubled sleep.

Three

It was sometime after dawn when a loud pounding awoke her. The insistence of the sound brought her completely awake.

Sitting up she called out, "What is it?"

"It's Rowen." His voice sounded urgent.

"Just a minute." She was already out of bed, slipping on her robe.

She murmured a spellword that released the energy stored in the rune she'd carved on the door, and it unlocked and opened.

Rowen stormed in. His spellstone glowed blue-white. His eyes searched her room anxiously.

Tim Fletcher followed and also looked around. His thin face was tight with tension.

"What is it?" she repeated.

Rowen ignored her and turned to Fletcher instead. "Go get Lord S'Carlton. I'm sure it's in here."

Fletcher nodded and was gone.

"What's here?"

Rowen continued to study the room.

"What's going on?" she asked again, grabbing his arm and facing him. His gray eyes, level with her own, looked worried.

"I've been searching the castle for the Shaltus-stone for several hours, gradually getting closer and closer to it. I think it's in here."

"Here?" Leah looked around her room in surprise.

How could the stone have been hidden in her room? Why would it be there?

She crossed to the windows and pulled open the curtains covering the narrow, glass-enclosed slits. Although the morning's light was warm and friendly, she felt a chill of foreboding.

Rowen was now circling the room like a caged animal, trying to sense the Shaltus-stone. Every so often he'd stop, pick up an object, study it, and then put it down.

"It can't be here!" Leah murmured.

She cupped her spellstone in her hands and focused on its amber depths. As she began a spell, the stone glowed warmly. The Shaltus-controlled presence was much stronger now, but try as she might she could not discover its origin. It seemed to pervade the entire castle with equal intensity.

Suddenly Rowen halted and placed his hands above the meter-high plant sitting on her desk. It was a skytree seedling, a recent present from her Sylvan grandfather. With a sinking feeling Leah remembered that she'd received it less than a week before she'd begun to feel the wrongness within the castle.

Rowen's hands slowly circled the seedling, moving lower until they rested on the large clay pot at its base. His fingers dug gently into the earth. Then his powerstone flared as he touched something. He pulled it out gingerly and rubbed the dirt off.

Lying on his palm was a dark spellstone about the size of a grape. It seemed to be a broken piece of a larger stone.

"How did it get there?" Leah asked in shock.

"You . . . you brought it here!" shouted a voice behind her.

She whirled to face her half-brother. His face was contorted with rage. Behind him stood Fletcher and several castle guards.

Leah shook her head in bewilderment. "No. Of course not."

"You're in league with Shaltus. You've sold out to help your Sylvie friends," Richard yelled.

"No!" Turning to Rowen, she shook her head. "No."

"Where did you get this plant?" asked Rowen. His eyes held no accusation.

"It was a present from my grandfather, Trask, chief of the Ayers tribe."

"You damn Sylvie traitor," shouted Richard, lunging forward to grab Leah and shake her.

"I didn't . . . and grandfather wouldn't have either," she yelled at him, while she struggled to free herself from his painful grip. Then Fletcher seized Richard's arm, and Rowen pulled Leah back away from him.

"My grandfather wants peace between the Sylvan and the humans," Leah said, gasping. She turned to Rowen. "He's tried to keep the treaty my father made—it's Richard who wants to break it. And the Sylvan would never join forces with anything as evil as the Shaltus-wraith. Someone else must have planted the stone here. . . ."

"We can discuss how the stone got here later," said Rowen as he stepped between Leah and her half-brother. "The important thing to do is to destroy it now. Because of Rusty's warning I started searching for the stone sooner than I normally would have. Its energy stores are still somewhat depleted. If I had waited, it would have been ready to attack by the time I found it. As it is . . ." He paused and smiled.

He clenched his amethyst-colored spellstone in his right hand. Then he pressed it against the Shaltus-controlled crystal in his left.

As the two stones met, the Shaltus-stone flashed like a ball of lightning. A blast of pain roared through

Leah's head. Richard gasped. His wristlet stones blazed with fire.

The lightning vanished.

Rowen's left hand now held only a charred lump that broke into scattered ashes as he spread his fingers. His own stone was apparently unharmed.

Suddenly the blood drained from his face. He staggered, fell forward, and crashed to the floor with a sickening thud.

Still reeling from the pain that throbbed through her head like thunder, Leah forced herself forward. She knelt beside the unconscious sorcerer. As he had aided her, she now helped him, pressing her hands against his to transfer energy to him. Concentrating on the link, she became oblivious to her surroundings and did not notice Fletcher kneel by her side.

She was equally unaware of her brother. His face flamed with anger and hatred.

She didn't hear him order the guards forward. She didn't notice them until they grabbed her and pulled her away from Rowen, breaking the link. Reality returned abruptly.

Richard was screaming at her.

"Get away from him. You traitor. You're just like your mother. Sylvie bitch! She bewitched my father, and she killed my mother!"

Richard's eyes blazed with a bitter fury that matched the tone of his voice. Evidently he blamed her for his own mother's death because his father had been visiting the Ayers forest to see his Sylvan lover when Shaltus had invaded Bluefield.

"That Sylvie killed my mother!" he repeated, stepping forward threateningly. Leah thought he was going to strike her, but instead he grabbed her arms and shook her violently.

"And my father brought you here. His Sylvie whelp." The acid in his voice shifted to the bitterness of envy. "You were his favorite, and all along you planned to betray us . . ."

"No. It's not true!" But he didn't seem to hear her words or see the pain in her face.

He twisted her arm roughly. "How did you get the stone in here? What does Shaltus plan to do? What did you sell out for?"

"I swear, I didn't have anything to do with it."

"Liar!"

Suddenly Leah realized that there was no way she could reason with her half-brother. There was madness in his eyes. It seemed that all the real and imagined hurts he had suffered through the years because of his mother's death and Leah's presence in the castle had built into a wall of hatred so fixed in his mind that it separated him from reality.

When he ordered one of the guards to prepare for her execution, she realized that some dark part of his mind had been waiting for an excuse for such an act for a long, long time.

"Take her down to the shielded cell," commanded Richard. It was a dungeon cell with silver walls to hold anyone with psychic powers. "The execution will take place at sunset."

As the guards started to move forward, Richard suddenly raised his hands to stop them. "I think I'd better take this first, though," he said, reaching for her spellstone.

Everything had happened too fast for Leah to plan what to do, but all her instincts for self-preservation reacted in that moment. When Richard's fingers touched her stone to pull it from her neck, she used its power.

A bolt of pure energy smashed into Richard, flinging him across the room. His body slammed into the wall, and he sagged senseless to the floor.

Startled, the guards reflexively loosened their grip.

THE SPELLSTONE OF SHALTUS 43

In that instant Leah pulled herself free and bolted through the door. Before they had a chance to dart after her, her magic slammed the door closed and locked the psi-activated rune-lock.

Then she was running down the hall, focusing all her strength into a shield that emanated from her stone and encircled her in an almost invisible golden aura of energy. She sensed that her blow had only knocked her half-brother unconscious. She knew that in moments he would be after her with his sorcery.

As she turned the corner to flee down the steps leading to the courtyard, she ran headlong into a heavyset man running up the stairs toward her. Her hand moved automatically to chop across the man's neck, but he seemed to know what she was going to do before she did and blocked her arm skillfully. Then she recognized him. It was Rusty.

"Wait a minute . . ." yelled the precog. "I know what happened . . ."

Something in his face prevented her from using her stone to knock him from her path.

"I've got horses ready for you . . ." He grabbed her arm and pulled her down the stairs after him.

There was no time to question him or to argue. All Leah could do was follow and be thankful that the precog was somehow on her side.

Fortunately the hallway below was deserted, and there were only a few soldiers in the courtyard. They looked on with surprise as Leah ran into the yard in her bathrobe, mounted her horse, and took the extra horse's reins that Rusty thrust into her hands.

Time was precious, but as he turned to leave she grabbed his shoulder.

"Why?"

His eyes held fear for her, and haste slurred his tongue. "Woke up and knew—too late to warn you— Rowen will know you're innocent, but he won't be able to convince your brother . . . You'll die today . . ."

The words froze her soul.

". . . Unless you go—now!"

His intense blue eyes commanded her more than his voice. Wordlessly she kicked her horse and galloped out of the gate.

Behind her she heard Rusty say something else. He could have meant a hundred things, but to Leah it seemed to be both a direction and an answer.

"The Sylvan. . . ."

Four

As Leah rode she tried to control her whirling thoughts and emotions. She had to be ready to fight Richard's magic when he regained consciousness, and she knew that that could happen at any minute. Her half-brother's range was about the same as her own, but his powers were somewhat greater. If she could only ride beyond his range before he woke up and oriented himself, she would be safe from his powers—at least for as long as she could maintain that distance—but somehow she sensed that that was not to be.

Still, it was difficult for her not to think about what had happened. How had the Shaltus-stone gotten into her room without her sensing it? Could it have lain dormant in the skytree pot while she carried the plant back to Castle Carlton? Could it have been powerful enough to obscure its hiding place even when she was in the same room with it? It didn't seem possible that she could have missed it; yet somehow it must have been so.

She had received the seedling less than a week before she'd felt the first glimmerings of the wrongness. And she had been in her room when she'd first sensed it. She hadn't been able to locate the stone even when Lord Rowen told her it was in her room. If the stone could conceal its presence from her when she was actively looking for it, it could have been hidden in her room for weeks.

If she had inadvertently brought the stone into the castle, it did seem likely that it had been planted in the skytree pot when she'd visited Ayers. She couldn't believe her grandfather had been responsible. Perhaps another Sylvan had hidden the stone.

She slowed her horses to a trot. They'd been galloping almost full out for the past four kilometers, and she couldn't afford to let them tire. Ayers was a normal day and a half's ride. She wondered whether she could make it in one long, very hard day's ride.

Since Richard thought she was working for the Sylvan, he'd guess that she would head there. He would send men after her without delay. Her only advantage was that she knew the infrequently used trails to the skytree forest far better than anyone else. She considered heading somewhere besides Ayers, but she had to find out the truth.

She had a chance as long as Richard wasn't close enough to track her with sorcery.

As she thought of her half-brother she felt a faint stirring. She had always been sensitive to her siblings, and they to her. Now she sensed that he was recovering consciousness.

Knowing that she could not win a one-to-one fight with him, she concentrated on protecting herself and her horses. The link with Lord Rowen had drained her strength. When Richard struck, however, his spells would have to travel a good-sized distance. He would have to expend far more energy in attacking than she would in defense.

She had not gone much farther down the trail when the attack began.

Bolts of energy burst around her. Sparks cascaded into the air as her shield absorbed and reflected the blows.

She lost control of her horses. They galloped ahead frantically and veered dangerously close to the trees lining the trail.

Although she did not have the strong telepathic powers that the Sylvan did over animals and plants, Leah had inherited a small measure of that power from her mother. Somewhat guiltily she used it now to calm and slow the horses. She forced them into a controlled gallop down the center of the path.

Her father had raised her as a human and had taught her human sorcery. He'd disapproved of her using the Sylvan ways. But as a child she'd sometimes secretly tried them.

The ground twisted and shook. It roared like a cyclone.

Clinging tightly to her saddle, Leah urged her horses forward. She felt certain that her mount would stumble, but somehow she found the will to keep going.

Ahead the earth cracked. She swerved to avoid the fissure. Trees fell to block her path. The horses jumped them or dodged.

Suddenly the road dipped. A massive fissure lay ahead.

It was too late to stop the horses. Leah kicked the mare hard with her bare feet. At the same time she mentally controlled both horses. They jumped.

For a moment she was aware of a deep gulf of raw earth beneath them—then the horses were on the other side. Her mount stumbled and slid on the edge of the crevice, trying to keep its footing on ground that would not hold still.

It lost its balance.

Having no choice, Leah diverted some of the energy from her shield to steady the ground.

Hooves dug frantically into loose soil and crumbling rock. The mare staggered, pulled away from the edge, and darted forward.

The other horse raced ahead of them. Leah released its mind from her control—she could not spare the energy.

Richard had been waiting for that moment. He struck again with lightninglike bolts. A few penetrated her inadequate shield before she could act. Fortunately the protective field dissipated most of the force, but several shafts reached her and her mare, burning into their skin like hot irons.

Leah channeled all her power back into the shield. The rest of the energy bolts fell harmlessly against it.

Suddenly the lightning vanished. For a moment Leah thought she was out of Richard's range. Then the trees ahead of her began to flame. She could not go back. There was no way through the thick forest except on the trail.

As smoke began to rise, she tightened her grip on the mare's mind so that it would not balk or waver. She intensified her shield. It became a wall of power capable of protecting her and the horse from fire and heat.

She didn't know who was more terrified, herself or her mount, but she tapped some inner reserve of willpower and forced her horse ahead.

Flaming branches and leaves surrounded them. Even with the shield she could smell the acrid smoke and feel the heat blasting them. The forest roared with a nightmare of fire.

She willed the horse onward. There had been a lot of rain over the past few days, and the amount of energy required to spread the fire would be enormous. It had to end soon.

Gasping for air, her mare slowed to a walk. While the shield kept out most of the smoke and heat, it also prevented fresh air from entering.

Abruptly the fire grew less intense. Leah sensed that Richard's power was weakening. They had almost reached the limit of his range.

Ahead fewer trees were burning. Then she was beyond the fire.

Reining her horse, Leah altered the shield to let in warm air that still smelled of smoke.

As Leah and the horse caught their breaths, the air on the trail ahead of them began to shift and coalesce into a thick mass that shimmered like desert air in the heat of day.

The outline of a huge beast glistened in the sun.

Leah looked up as the monster solidified. It was vaguely manlike in shape, but over four meters tall. The face had no features except for a wide, slavering mouth filled with huge teeth. Four long arms ended in taloned hands.

Automatically she clamped down on her frightened mount's mind before the horse reared. She sensed that the beast was Richard's last weapon; beyond it she would be out of his range.

The strain of shielding herself and the horses for the last kilometer had weakened Leah's defenses. She knew that she would not have enough strength to continue to protect herself and her horse.

The monster lumbered toward her on two massive legs. Its strangely smooth gray skin glittered with unnatural luminescence.

If she used the shield to protect herself, her horse would die. Without the horse she could never outrun Richard's men. She had to fight.

As the beast of air and magic bore down upon her, she murmured a spell that transferred all her power into a weapon. Her shield vanished.

A long, thin sword of pure energy appeared in her hand. Its handle looked like glass; its blade seemed as insubstantial as a sunbeam.

Leah had no great skill with a sword. However, she had received the same minimal training in the martial arts that every child did. She hoped that her choice of defense would surprise Richard.

As she swung the sword, her mind maneuvered the horse.

The giant twisted to avoid her blade. It clawed at her mount as it turned. But her mental command sent the horse into an unexpected backstep so that the monster's taloned hands clutched at empty air.

Her sword whistled back toward the beast in a feint. Its upper arms reached to block it, while its lower pair of arms caught her waist in a vise grip. Then her blade swerved suddenly, blazed like a white hot flame, and rammed into the beast's chest.

Although talons dug into her sides and tried to drag her from her horse, Leah poured every ounce of strength she had left into the blade, which was now buried up to its hilt in the thing's chest.

At the point of the sword's entry the beast began to dissolve. In seconds nothing was left except the two great arms that still held her. She was screaming now as the talons tore through her thin clothing and into her flesh, but she continued to recite the spell. Finally even the arms disappeared.

Without the pressure of the beast's claws on her body she slumped forward. The spellsword fell from her grasp, vanishing instantly.

Leah almost lost consciousness as pain and fatigue overwhelmed her. Released from her mental control, her terrified horse dashed down the trail at breakneck speed. It took all of Leah's will to keep from blacking out as she brought the horse to a standstill. But there was no time to rest—she had to keep moving before Richard started after her. She was out of his range now, but with fresh horses he could soon catch up with her.

Recalling that food could be a substitute for rest, she quickly dismounted and searched the saddlebags, praying that Rusty had packed some supplies. Fortunately there was a large packet of beef jerky and some journeycakes made of honey, nuts, and rolled oats, as well as a canteen of water. She also found a packet of salve.

She examined her wounds. The beast's talons had raked long gashes on her waist and stomach. Although the wounds were painful, they were not very deep. She spread the ointment over them and used strips of cloth torn from her tattered bathrobe as crude bandages. Then she tended to her mount's needs. The horse had only a few scratches and several minor burns. She used the last of the salve on its injuries and gave it some of the water.

She remounted and prodded the horse back into a trot. Although she felt numb with exhaustion, she forced herself to eat several of the journeycakes as she rode. When she finished she sagged forward, letting her head rest against the mare's neck.

For a long while she expected to feel Richard's magic stir around her. But as the minutes grew into hours and no attack came, she guessed that he'd expended too much energy to renew the attack immediately. He must have decided to rest before setting out after her. Of course, he'd probably already sent out a party of soldiers, but as long as she could stay outside of Richard's range there was a good chance of eluding them.

The land between Castle Carlton and Ayers was a deep forest broken only by a maze of hunting trails and animal tracks. After Richard's attack ended Leah turned off the main road to Ayers at the first opportunity. In the hours that followed she steered her horse over a variety paths and trails on a route that would not be easy to follow. Despite the temptation to go to her father's old hunting cabin, where she could obtain food, clothing, and shelter, Leah bypassed it and headed farther south. The cabin was just off the main road, and her half-brother would undoubtedly expect her to go there.

Unfortunately the spare horse had vanished during the fire, so she reduced her pace considerably to conserve her mare's strength. It was now apparent that she would never make it in a single day's ride.

As her horse trotted slowly along the little-used trails, Leah fell into an exhausted daze. She remained aware enough to guide her horse, yet later found that she could not remember the ride or understand how she had had the strength to keep going.

When the elongated shadows of evening made it almost too dark to see the rough track, she halted the horse in a thick glade of oaks. Feeding the mare the last of the journeycakes and most of the water, she studied the darkening forest.

The quiet calm of the shadowed glade seemed inviting and somehow secure.

Leah suddenly wondered if perhaps she could use her Sylvan heritage to advantage. Her father had forbidden her to use what little Sylvan power she'd inherited. He'd wanted her to be accepted as human. When she'd shown signs of having human as well as Sylvan psychic abilities, he'd given her a spellstone and trained her with her half-brother. But as a child she'd sometimes secretly tried to imitate the powers she saw used during her brief, infrequent visits to the Sylvan forest.

Still, her efforts at animal mind control were successful only at close range, and she'd soon grown tired of the game of "taming" a squirrel or rabbit. When she'd tried the Sylvan skill of shaping living trees and plants and controlling their growth, it had taken so much effort and time to see any bending of a branch that she'd given up after one or two tries.

Now it occurred to her that, since she was able to shape a little, perhaps she could also draw some strength from trees as the Sylvan did. Of course, they normally drew on the energy stored in the enormous skytrees, but she'd heard that any tree could be tapped. She couldn't remember ever having tested that ability, but she was exhausted enough to make it worth a try.

She walked to the largest oak, pressed her hands and face against its trunk, and focused her mind on it. Slowly she felt herself merging with the tree as she had during a shaping. But instead of trying to enforce her will upon its structure to effect some change, she concentrated on blending with it to draw upon its strength.

She found it surprisingly easy to merge her mind with the tree's being. She quickly became submerged in its calm strength and infinite peace.

It was overpowering, narcotic, and anesthetizing.

Five

Leah awoke as the eastern sky began to brighten with predawn light. She lay slumped against the bottom of the oak with her arms still embracing its trunk. Gently drawing away, she rolled onto her back and yawned.

Above her the oak soared into the sky. Through the tenuous link that remained she could feel the tree waken to the rising sun, gradually turn its leaves toward the east, and begin to feed on the sunlight.

She felt completely relaxed and at ease; the tree's serenity had become her own. A feeling of well-being, which a few hours of mere sleep alone could not have produced, had replaced her terrible fatigue. Even the pain of her wounds was diminished.

Perhaps she really was more Sylvan than human. Maybe that was why she'd never been accepted by the people at Carlton or had really liked her life there. She'd always felt more attuned to the simple, close-to-nature life in the Sylvan forests than to the more complex civilization in Carlton and in the other Eastern Kingdoms.

For a moment she rested and savored her surroundings, watching the pink-frosted cirrus clouds drift eastward, feeling the warm summer breeze tickle her face, listening to the symphony of waking birds, smelling the dew-laden grass and moss. She was glad to be outside, away from confining castle walls.

Reluctantly she severed her bond with the tree.

Now that the tree's spell was broken, a measure of anxiety encroached on the lingering feeling of serenity. She had slept longer than she had intended. She had to keep moving.

She took several sips of water and gave the rest to her horse, saddled it, and mounted. Since there were no more journeycakes, she breakfasted on the beef jerky. It was dry, salty, and tough, but she was so hungry that she almost enjoyed it.

When she finished she concentrated on her spellstone. It glowed eagerly in response. The sleep and tree-tap had restored most of her power. She focused through the stone and searched to the limit of her range for pursuers, but the forest was clear. They were probably still behind her and searching farther to the north.

As she guided the mare along the trail toward the Ayers forest, Leah began to mull over all that had happened.

It did seem likely that the Shaltus-stone had been planted in the pot with her skytree seedling. Apparently she'd unknowingly brought the crystal into Carlton. Still, she couldn't believe that her grandfather had been involved.

Trask had always been kind to her, even encouraging her to visit him, when the other Sylvan in his tribe were against it. Moreover, he was one of the few Sylvan who kept working for peace between the forest people and their human neighbors.

Leah thought about the long-standing enmity between the Sylvan and the humans. Although each race believed the other to be alien and inferior, they were probably both of the same species.

Her father had taught her that the Sylvan were human despite their physical differences. As proof he pointed out that the two groups could interbreed and produce offspring, although it was rare. Of course, the half-Sylvan males, called *shiffmen* by the Sylvan, were sterile, but the half-Sylvan females, *shiffem*, were not.

Her father had told her that long ago, perhaps thousands and thousands of years, there had only been humans. Then the god N'Omb had descended to earth to punish man for his sins. There had been a tremendous civilization, but the people had tried to unlock the secrets of the universe with knowledge reserved for N'Omb. N'Omb destroyed most of them and their civilization, even changing the shape of the world. During the process many things, including plants and animals, were altered. Some men became Sylvan. Some plants evolved into skytrees.

The official view of the N'Omb Church was similar, except it held that the most evil men were changed into the Sylvan and condemned to live in skytrees. Thus the Sylvan were to be shunned and despised. They were something alien—no longer human.

The Sylvan did not believe in N'Omb. According to Sylvan legends, their god *Shuull* lived deep within the earth. He had blessed the Sylvan and lifted them above common men. The skytrees were *Shuull's* mightiest creations. They were also divine conduits to the god himself. When the Sylvan drew energy from the trees they were receiving power directly from *Shuull*. If *Shuull* had divinely blessed the Sylvan, then conversely he had also divinely cursed the humans.

With such legends it was no wonder that humans and Sylvan hated one another. But more than legend or racial prejudice was involved in the feud.

For one thing, skytree forests were widely scattered. Most were located within boundaries of the states making up the Eastern Kingdoms. There had been a history of border disputes and all sorts of squabbles about trade, hunting rights, and the like.

The huge skytrees themselves were a major cause of contention. Their sap could be processed into a healing drug called *tomaad*. Not only was *tomaad* almost a cure-all, but it could also greatly reduce the fatigue produced by sorcery, making it tremendously valuable. However, the *tomaad* sap and *delaap* nuts from the skytrees were the main staples of the Sylvan diet. In fact, the Sylvan were dependent on them and would die if deprived for more than a short period of time.

The Sylvan considered skytree products to be sacred food from *Shuull*. As a result the Sylvan would not sell or trade *tomaad*. They even refused to trade valuable skytree wood, which could produce huge pieces of beautiful, durable lumber.

Greed had been the stimulus for raids and border wars. But the Sylvan's psychic abilities were generally powerful enough to prevent invasion. That was one reason why it was so hard to believe that any Sylvan would join forces with the Shaltus-wraith—the Sylvan were powerful enough that they thought they didn't need any allies to protect their forests from humans.

Leah wondered if Rusty's precognition had disclosed how the Shaltus-stone had been planted in the castle. Just how comprehensive were his abilities?

Even if he'd been sure of her innocence, why had he gone out of his way to save her? Had he now put himself in jeopardy with her half-brother? Or had he decided by now that he'd made a mistake in helping a Sylvie, and could he, would he, use his precognitive ability to help Richard's men find her?

She wondered what Michael Rowen was doing. Would he really trust his precog friend's judgment of her innocence, or would he side with Richard?

She remembered the way Rowen had acted toward her. It had been as though he'd accepted her for what she was, seeing her as a person, not as a Sylvan half-

breed. Fletcher and Rusty apparently had the same
attitude. But everything had happened so fast—perhaps she had only imagined it.

Still, Lord Rowen had seemed genuinely concerned
when she'd fainted, even to the point of using his
energy reserves to give her strength.

She remembered the way he'd pressed his hands
against hers. They were such large hands. She could
visualize them as well as she could his face. Deeply
tanned skin, long fingers with a wide reach, roughened
palms from riding, his right hand calloused from
fencing. Powerful hands, yet capable of gentleness.

Now that she had time to think about it, it occurred
to her that Michael Rowen was really a rather handsome man.

She couldn't blame Barbara for being interested in
him. She wondered, with more than a little envy, how
her half-sister was doing. By now both she and Rowen
had probably recovered from the effects of the
Shaltus-stone. Leah had a feeling that they would be
getting along quite well.

She frowned. The image of Barbara with Rowen
was surprisingly unpleasant.

Determinedly she pushed the thought out of her
mind and concentrated on her surroundings.

While she'd been daydreaming, her horse had
traveled a good distance. They had almost reached the
Twelvepeople River.

At the river she turned north on a narrow trail that
ran alongside it. Eventually small skytrees appeared.
Soon the skytrees dominated the forest, pushing out
stunted oaks and pines.

The skytrees became enormous. They towered to
heights of sixty to ninety meters and more, their trunks
ranging from ten to twenty meters wide. Their enormous branches and meter-wide leaves blotted out the
sun, turning the summer's day into deep twilight.

Little else but fungus and moss grew beneath their impenetrable cover. A thick brown carpet of leaves cushioned the sound of the mare's hooves.

The forest's unnatural stillness and darkness would have been frightening to most visitors, but Leah felt at peace, as though she were coming home. Although she had spent all her life at Castle Carlton, she had been out of place within its walls. She felt as though she belonged among the huge skytrees.

Yet at her birth the Sylvan had declared her an outcast. As a *shiffem* she was not welcome. Only her grandfather had welcomed her visits. Now that her half-brother had condemned her to death could she really expect to find sanctuary with the Sylvan?

Leah's stomach twisted into a knot. What would she do if Trask refused her refuge? Where could she go? Her mouth felt dry, there was a lump in her throat, and for the first time in a long time she felt on the verge of tears. Long ago she'd learned to hide her feelings, to bury the pain of rejection deep inside, to face the world with a mask of indifference.

No. With stubborn determination she drew a ragged breath and fought back the tears. For the moment she was here, and she had to find out who had planted the Shaltus-stone. That was the important thing. She would worry about the future after she'd seen her grandfather. Until then she had to appear calm and confident; the Sylvan would respect nothing else.

Resolutely she smoothed her long, tangled hair and adjusted her torn robe. Her attire embarrassed her, but there had been no spare clothes in her saddlebag. Summoning all her courage, she prodded her horse into a trot.

Long before she reached the heart of the forest Leah felt the presence of the Sylvan. She was sure that unseen lookouts watched. She had never entered the forest from this direction before, but it seemed as well guarded as her usual route.

She clamped a tight shield over her thoughts against telepathic probes. Although most Sylvan were not telepaths, there were enough who were that she would keep her mind barricaded as long as she stayed within the skytree forest.

Suddenly two Sylvan guards swung down on ropes suspended· from branches high in the trees. As they dropped from their ropes to block her path, Leah halted and dismounted.

She knew one of the Sylvan; he was called Curlov. Both were thin, muscular men, well over two meters tall. As she towered over most humans, they towered above her.

They had shoulder-length silver-green hair pulled behind their heads and tied back. Fine body-hair gave their light skin a soft greenish tinge. Their large, mismatched colored eyes with enlarged pupils gave them better sight in the forest's dim interior. The nails on their bare feet and their thin fingers were long and clawlike. Otherwise their physical appearance was no different from that of humans.

They wore loose, thigh-length tunics made of *dolaan*, a soft clothlike material made from specially treated skytree leaves. Curlov's tunic had been dyed dark brown and was decorated with leaf designs. The other man's garment had been left natural green, but its cuffs were trimmed with squirrel fur.

"Leahdes, what are you doing here? We had no word that you were expected," said Curlov. Although the Sylvan language was almost identical to the human, it was spoken with a distinctive, lilting accent.

Curlov looked curiously at her tattered clothes but made no comment.

Straightening her shoulders, Leah stared back defiantly.

"My visit is unexpected, but that is no business of yours. I am here to see Trask," she paused and added "my grandfather." Her voice had slipped naturally into Sylvan dialect.

"You cannot see him now. Our chief is ill." From the way he stressed "our" it was clear that he meant to exclude Leah.

Forcing back a surge of panic, she calmly asked, "What happened to Trask? When I was here several weeks ago he was fine."

Curlov nodded. There was a solemnity about his face that frightened her.

"No one knows. He fell ill suddenly, and even *tomaad* does not help."

"I want to see him." There were few conditions that *tomaad* could not cure. Her grandfather had to be seriously ill indeed.

"I will take you to Quinen. He is in charge now."

Leah's eyebrows arched upward in surprise. Although Quinen was Trask's foster son, he'd often opposed Trask's policies. She had not realized that he had enough backing in the tribal council to become second in command. But it would be good to see Quinen again. She hadn't seen him in months. He'd always treated her well, at times with an almost brotherly affection.

Her lips curved into a slight smile as she pictured his handsome, boyish features.

Then Curlov gestured toward the other Sylvan. "Come now. Stukis will take care of your horse."

Leah nodded, handed the other the reins, and followed Curlov to the ropes.

Unseen Sylvan, manning a pulley system fastened to one of the enormous branches high above, pulled her swiftly aloft. As the line whistled upward, meter-wide leaves brushed against her legs and arms, and small twigs jabbed at her. At the end was a platform shaped from a branch about thirty meters from the ground.

At this height the forest was a fantastic world of its own, alien to and isolated from the land below. Masses of dark green foliage hid the earth and all that was connected to it. Giant trunks soared toward a sky that was still obscured by immense branches, intertwining boughs, and oversized leaves. Between the unseen blue of sky and brown of earth there was only the green of trees stretching as far as the eye could see.

Following Curlov toward the bole of the mammoth tree, Leah took a deep breath of sweet, skytree-blossom-scented air and sighed. It was good to be here. Whether it was some effect of her melding with the oak or merely a reaction of her Sylvan heritage, she felt a strong sense of belonging.

Curlov led the way through a knothole into the interior of the tree and up a six-meter ladder that had been psychically shaped rather than carved in the living wood. They exited through another hole on the opposite side of the trunk and climbed a rope ladder to a crossing branch. This bough had been shaped into a flattened walkway. After crossing to several other branches and ascending a second ladder, they reached the edge of the Sylvan village, some sixty meters above the ground.

The village consisted of dozens of airy treehouses built onto limbs and numerous homes built into the trunks and branches themselves. Some of the branches had been shaped to form large rounded rooms with symmetrical knotholes for doors and windows. Knots large enough for doors and small portholes dotted the trunks. Suspension bridges, ropes, and ladders connected the trees.

Shafts of sunlight streamed through the thinned foliage above the multilevel village to sparkle off metal decorations embedded in the walls and bridges. Pastel-shaded paint on the outside structures broke the forest's green monotony.

Leah grabbed Curlov's arm as the Sylvan escorted her across a bridge and into the guest room shaped inside one of the lower branches.

"When can I see Trask?"

"I do not believe that will be possible at this time, but I will inform Quinen that you are here," Curlov replied. "Remain in this room until he sends for you."

"Can you arrange to have some food sent up, and some fresh clothes?"

For the first time a trace of emotion crossed the Sylvan's face as he looked amused. But he said nothing about her disheveled garb. "I can. . ."

"Thank you, Curlov, I'd appreciate that."

The Sylvan nodded and left.

Leah glanced around the room. It was sparsely furnished with a fur-covered sleeping pallet, a couple of chairs, a set of shelves, and a large table shaped from the living skytree. Behind an arched door lay a bathroom complete with tub, sink, and toilet, all shaped from the tree. Its roots supplied warm water from hot springs as well as cold from underground rivers. The tree used the waste water as a source of nutrients.

Eventually a Sylvan woman brought the requested food and clothing, including a glass of *tomaad*. Leah drank the liquid immediately. In a few moments the pain from her wounds and her body's soreness from the strenuous ride vanished. Then she ate the meal of skytree nut bread and a salad of mushrooms, vegetables, *delaap* nuts, and herbs.

The Sylvan did not eat much in the way of meat—a bit of squirrel and venison, but that was about all. Leah found herself wishing for some beef or fowl to go with the meal, and that made her wonder just how much of a home the Ayers forest would be—if she were allowed to stay. She was Sylvan enough to prefer living close to nature, but there were some things about the simple, almost primitive life-style that she might never get used to. The primarily vegetarian diet was only one aspect.

After eating, she bathed and dressed. She'd been given a light tunic of unadorned *dolaan* that reached to her knees. There were no undergarments, and it was just as well, for she vastly preferred the loose Sylvan mode of dress to the stiff corsets and layers of underclothes required by human custom. Yet the *dolaan* was coarse and uncomfortable compared to human-spun cotton.

As she bound her hair, Sylvan-style, in a single braid along the side of her face, she began to feel more anxious. What could have happened to her grandfather? Was it only coincidence that he had fallen ill just as the Shaltus-wraith attacked Carlton, or was there some sinister connection?

With a worried frown Leah cupped her spellstone in her hands and probed for any trace of the wraith's influence. She sensed nothing abnormal. There was no sign of any Shaltus-programmed stone or any indication that one had ever been in Ayers. But if a Sylvan had not planted the stone in her skytree pot, who had?

Impatiently she paced the round room until the quiet of evening descended on the forest.

She wondered what would happen if Quinen became chief. Although he had been kind to her, she knew that Quinen had a deep hatred of humans. Trask had raised Quinen after his parents were killed in a human raid. Recently he'd become the leader of a group of young dissidents in the Ayers tribe that wanted war. As chief, could Quinen garner enough support to start a war with Carlton?

Tired of waiting for Quinen's summons Leah

stalked out of the room and headed for Trask's chambers. She had to know her grandfather's condition.

When she reached the door to Trask's rooms she found two burly Sylvan men guarding it.

"No one is allowed in there," said one as he blocked her entrance.

"I'm Leahdes Carlton. Trask is my grandfather."

"We have our orders."

"And whose orders are they? I might be able to help Trask."

"My orders," said a voice behind her.

She whirled and found herself facing the *Shuull* priest, Geraed. He wore a floor-length robe of bleached-white *dolaan* over a calf-length tunic of the same material. A single line of scarlet paint across his forehead marked his position as head priest of the tribe.

"I believe you were told to wait in your room," said Geraed.

"I think I waited long enough. I want to see Trask."

"Very well, you may see him. Then we'll have a little talk, and you'll explain just why you are here."

The priest gestured at the guard. As the man moved away from the door, Geraed seized Leah's arm and marched her into Trask's suite. He didn't release her until they reached the bedroom, and Leah stood in front of Trask's bed.

The bed was an oval platform rising out of the floor. Like most of the furniture in Sylvan skytrees, it was a shaped part of the tree. There were leaf designs around its base and on the edge of the headboard, which grew out of the wall. The elaborate pattern appeared to have been carved, but on closer inspection it was clear that it had been shaped by Sylvan powers.

In the center of the bed lay an old man who was obviously near death.

Leah stared at Trask in stunned silence. It was hard to believe that he was the same man she had visited only a few weeks before. He looked withered, shriveled. His skin had turned from pale white to the brown of a long dead leaf. Most of his silver-green hair had fallen out. There was only a fringe of it left to frame a face of hollow cheeks and sunken eyes. It was almost impossible to believe that any natural illness could have ravaged a robust man of sixty so quickly.

"What happened?" Her words were half-sob, half-whisper.

"We don't know. He was fine until a week and a half ago. He went to bed, apparently normal, but the next morning his servents found him unconscious on the floor. Since then his condition has degenerated. *Tomaad* has not helped, and our healers have found neither cause or cure. He's in a coma now. I'm sorry."

"Maybe there is something I can do."

As Leah pulled out her spellstone and began to kneel at Trask's side, Geraed grabbed her arm and pulled her upright.

"You will not use your human magic on our chief."

Although the priest was about average height for a Sylvan, he was still more than thirty centimeters taller than Leah. As he towered over her, his mere physical presence was as intimidating as the tone of his voice.

"But maybe my sorcery could do something to help him," she protested weakly.

"No. It is for *Shuull* to aid him." His voice was as unyielding as his hand, which yanked her around to face the door.

Then the door opened and a tall Sylvan entered. His handsome face was totally masked by a rather savage-looking design of paint. It was difficult to read the expression on his face, but his mismatched eyes of gray and brown looked warmly at Leah. It was Quinen.

Leah was glad to see him, but the paint he wore dismayed her. It identified him as the chief of the tribe. Evidently the Sylvan thought Trask's death was inevitable.

Normally Quinen wore paint only on his right cheek to represent his position as the head communicator of the Ayers tribe. The communicators were telepaths with fantastic range. They linked the isolated skytree forests. Now his left cheek was painted to show that he had taken over Trask's duties as the master tree-shaper, and designs on his forehead and nose indicated his position as chief of the tribe.

"You were to wait in your room until I sent for you," said Quinen, interrupting Leah's thoughts.

"I wanted to see my grandfather. I've told Geraed that I may be able to help him, using my spellstone, but he objected. Surely it couldn't hurt to try."

The priest frowned. "If *Shuull's* power could not aid him, there is nothing your human magic could do."

Quinen nodded. "Geraed has done his best, but I'm afraid there is nothing more to be done. I'm sorry, Leahdes."

"But human magic is different from Sylvan power," Leah objected. "It is as if one were rain and the other snow; though they are both of the same substance, they have different properties. Perhaps there is something I can accomplish that Sylvan cannot."

Geraed objected, "That is sacrilege. *Shuull's* powers are far greater than human magic."

"But if there is nothing more that you can do, what harm would there be for me to try?"

The Sylvan priest shook his head doubtfully. He walked over to Trask and studied the chief's emaciated face. Geraed's expression became grave.

He turned back toward Leah. "He is dying, and

there is nothing I can do. All right. It cannot hurt for you to try."

Now it was Quinen's turn to look angry. "But it is human magic. Surely we cannot entrust Trask's life to it."

Geraed studied Quinen's irate expression thoughtfully. "I would have thought that you would be willing to try anything to save your foster-father."

"Anything but human magic—a minute ago you were against it too."

"Until I realized that Trask is truly dying."

"But not human magic—it is dangerous, evil . . .

The priest was looking at Quinen suspiciously. "Do you suspect Leahdes's motives? She may be only a *shiffem*, but she is of Trask's blood, and I do not believe she would do anything to endanger his life."

"Of course not, but . . ."

Geraed's voice took on a note of sarcasm. "And naturally you would not want to overlook any chance of aiding Trask. After all, if he were to die, you would be the one forced to assume his responsibilities. I know how reluctant you are to become chief . . ."

Beneath his mask of paint Quinen's face turned a shade redder.

"Naturally we must do all we can to aid Trask. All right, if you are certain there is nothing more you can do, we'll let Leahdes try her magic. But I do not think it will do any good."

Leah sighed with relief. She didn't know if she would be able to accomplish anything, but she had to try. While she was not one of the sorcerers especially gifted in the healing arts, she had been given basic training in that area. So she hoped she would be able to determine at least the cause of Trask's mysterious illness, if not to effect an immediate cure.

Once again she knelt at Trask's side. She removed her powerstone from around her neck, placed the

crystal over Trask's heart, and concentrated on it
while she recited a spell. Gradually she entered a
trancelike state. As she probed Trask's body psychically, she seemed to see alternating images on the
back of her closed eyelids—first his skeleton, then his
organs, the circulatory and nervous systems, and the
muscular tissue.

She stretched her arms out and passed her hands
over his body from head to toe and back. She began
to sense the wrongness. There were several distur-
bances—small stones in one of the kidneys, a twisted
bone in his right arm from a childhood fall, scar tissue
along his chest and on the side of one lung from old
wounds. But these were minor compared to the
wrongness that seemed to be everywhere.

Poison.

She did not have the skill or the training to determine what kind it was, and it had spread too far to
destroy with sorcery. She did the only thing she could
—she channeled energy into the frail body and prayed
that it would give the old chief enough strength to
fight off the venom on his own.

Then she broke the rapport.

"Well?" said the priest.

She swung around and surveyed the two men
critically. Could either of them have been involved?

"Trask has been poisoned," she said.

"What?" Quinen's surprise seemed genuine.

Geraed's eyes widened, but he said nothing.

"Unfortunately there's nothing I can do to determine the kind of poison. I've transferred energy to
Trask, but I don't know if it will do any good."

The priest gazed down at Trask. "He looks somewhat better. There's more color in his cheeks, and his
breathing is more regular."

"It may be that I did help him, but the effects
could be only temporary."

Quinen frowned. His mask of paint seemed to twist his lips into a grimace. "I'll send for some guards. If someone has tried to poison Trask, they could try again."

"That won't be necessary," said the priest. "That's why I've had my men stationed outside the door. I suspected this."

"What?" Quinen glared at the *Shuull* priest. "You suspected that Trask was poisoned and didn't tell anyone?"

"I didn't know whom I could trust."

"Are you implying that I'm involved?"

Geraed said nothing, and his silence was an answer.

"What about you? How do we know you didn't arrange this? You were the last one to see Trask that night, if you'll remember. And you and your healers haven't done a thing to help Trask."

Geraed smiled without humor. "That's really a rather amusing theory. You also saw him that night. And who has the most to gain by our chief's death? You've never agreed with Trask's policy toward humans. You're the one who's tried to oust him as chief. You had enough support to be made second in command, but Trask was in too strong a position to be removed by anything except illness . . . or death."

Quinen's indignation was plain. "That's ridiculous. Trask's been like a father to me, you know that. Even if we didn't agree on things, even if I did want to become chief, I couldn't hurt him."

Leah wondered if Quinen was sincere; he certainly seemed to be. She'd always liked him, and she wanted to believe him. Yet she knew that in recent years his hatred of humans had put him in direct opposition to Trask's pacifist views. The two had grown far apart. But it didn't seem possible that Quinen would have attempted to murder Trask.

"I certainly have no reason to poison Trask," Geraed retorted.

"These accusations aren't getting us anywhere," interjected Leah. "You two aren't the only ones who had the opportunity to poison my grandfather, and there are others who might have reason. Maybe this has something to do with the Shaltus-wraith. . . ."

"Shaltus? Why would he bother us?" asked Quinen. "And how could he do anything at this range?"

"I don't know, but he was able to plant a programmed spellstone at Carlton," replied Leah.

She told them what happened at the castle.

"Your brother thinks the Sylvan have joined Shaltus?" said Geraed in a shocked voice when she had finished. "A human-wraith is no friend of ours."

"Then how did that spellstone get into a skytree plant that I'd gotten from Trask?"

Quinen's mismatched eyes looked thoughtful. "Perhaps some human planted it there after you'd reached the castle. Who better to blame than a *shiffem?*"

"But no human could have poisoned my grandfather, and it seems far too much of a coincidence for this to have happened at this time. Perhaps Shaltus knows something of the enmity between humans and Sylvan. Maybe he knows that if Trask dies Quinen will become the chief and that there would probably be a war between the Sylvan and Carlton—and that would be to Shaltus's advantage."

"Aren't you giving Shaltus a bit too much credit?" replied Quinen. "How could he know what we are doing? We're talking about Shaltus as though he were still alive. But 'he' is really an it, a wraith, and a wraith has certain limitations, including nonmobility."

Leah nodded. "But if he—it—has a Sylvan under control . . ."

"Don't you think we'd be able to sense that?" asked the priest.

"Perhaps not. Sylvans cannot usually detect human sorcery, and the wraith was human once. We really don't know much about a wraith's abilities anyway. And I'm not overlooking the possibility that some Sylvan could be involved willingly." Leah studied the two men.

Quinen's painted face was unreadable. "But no Sylvan would willingly ally himself with a human wraith." He turned toward Geraed. "We are overlooking an important aspect of what Leahdes has told us. Richard S'Carlton believes that our tribe is allied with Shaltus. Even though it is not true, if he thinks it is, he might decide to declare war against us. I think the important thing to do right now is to make some preparations for defense."

"We can send a message to S'Carlton and try to convince him that the Sylvan are not involved," said Geraed. "We'd better convene the tribal council and decide what's to be done. We also have to decide what to do about Leahdes. She may be Trask's granddaughter, but she is still a *shiffem*, and she cannot become part of the tribe. Perhaps if we send her back to S'Carlton, it will show our goodwill. . . ."

Before Leah could protest, Quinen put his hand protectively on her shoulder and spoke.

"No. We cannot send Leahdes back to Carlton. Who knows what her brother might do if she were to return. Perhaps he has cooled down by now and has realized that she would not help Shaltus. Or he might realize it if she were to return. But we have no way of knowing that. Leahdes may have human blood, but she is also our chief's granddaughter, and we must protect her."

Leah looked gratefully at Quinen.

"It will be for the council to decide," he continued. "And there have been cases where *shiffems* were readmitted to the tribe. Certainly she can remain for a few days while we try to sort this all out."

Geraed's disapproval was plain, but he said nothing.

"Thank you," said Leah, her voice almost a sigh of relief.

"Now I think you'd better go back to your room, Leahdes. You've done what you can for Trask. Geraed and I have things to discuss."

Quinen squeezed her shoulder gently. The gesture seemed both affectionate and possessive.

"All right." Leah stared at the two men for a moment more, searching for some answer in their face to the still unexplained sequence of events that had brought her here. Then she sighed, for there were no answers, only more questions.

Reluctantly she turned away and headed back to her room.

Six

Leah spent the next few days at Trask's side. Although she transferred energy to him each day, his condition failed to improve. He never stirred from the deep coma.

She saw nothing of Quinen or Geraed and was told that they were both busy at council meetings.

Then on the evening of the fifth day there was a sharp knock on her door.

"Come in," she called, glancing up from the garment she was sewing. She had been given several tunics and a pair of trousers but had to alter them. She was not as tall or thin as the average Sylvan female. She also had a new pair of light deerskin boots for riding; like the Sylvan she would remain barefoot in the tree-tops.

Quinen strode into the room. Closing the door quietly behind him, he said, "I hope I'm not disturbing you."

"Not at all." Leah smiled at him. She was glad to see that he no longer wore his painted mask of authority. This was evidently a social visit rather than an official one.

Without the savage covering his face was quite handsome, with well-shaped features and almost boyish good looks. It was quite a contrast to the harshness that the paint had imposed. Only his eyes were unchanged—the mismatched eyes of silver and topaz showed a keen intelligence, but with a coldness about them that disturbed Leah.

She remembered a time many years before when his eyes always seemed full of good humor. Then there had been a series of raids against various Sylvan forests that had reminded Quinen of his parents' death. The disagreements with his foster-father, Trask, had intensified. She had not seen much of him after that—he'd been sent to another forest for advanced training as a communicator, and her visits to the Ayers forest had become less frequent—but from what she had seen the intervening years had only increased the bitterness in his eyes.

"I thought you might want some company," he said.

"I'd like that. I've hardly spoken to anyone in the last few days."

"Oh, I've brought you something," said Quinen, pulling his hand from behind his back. In it was a bottle of *dinuuci*, a sweet liquor made from fermented *delaap* nuts.

Leah laughed as he handed it to her. "I remember the last time you gave me some of this."

The big Sylvan grinned, and his eyes seemed to soften. "When was that? Five, six years ago? You've grown up since then."

"More like about seven years," Leah replied. "I must have been an awful nuisance. Grandfather had invited me to spend a whole month with him, the longest I've ever spent here."

"And then he was called away on some business or other, leaving me in charge of you," added Quinen.

"I was just a kid then, about twelve years old, and I tagged along after you unmercifully. You were about seventeen. You were pretty disgusted at being saddled with a brat like me."

Quinen nodded. "You followed me around and copied everything I did."

"I guess I thought that if I could be more like you Trask would be proud of me." Leah laughed again. "Then you decided to get back at me for being such a pest, and you offered me some of the *dinuuci* you were drinking. I guess I learned not to copy you—I got drunk, passed out, and oh was I sick the next day."

Quinen grinned sheepishly. "I guess it wasn't very nice of me." His voice grew more serious as his eyes caught hers and held them. "I got a little drunk too."

Leah blushed and abruptly turned away to study the almost empty shelves in the back of the room. "I think I've got some glasses here," she said, going over to the shelves to look.

She remembered what had happened only vaguely, but she knew that sometime during that night she'd found Quinen's arm around her shoulders and that they'd shared several long and rather intense kisses. They'd never mentioned the incident again, and she'd almost forgotten it. Suddenly she felt certain Quinen had not.

"Here we are," she said, taking two small, brown glasses from the shelf. Avoiding Quinen's gaze, she took them back over to the table and poured the liquor. As she handed him one glass, she changed the subject.

"This waiting hasn't been easy. Has the tribal council decided anything about my staying in Ayers?"

Quinen pulled up a chair, shrugged, and sat down at the table. "Not yet. But it looks like the council won't force you to return to Carlton. They are still discussing under what conditions you'd be allowed to remain in Ayers. Meanwhile, they've sent a message to Lord S'Carlton denying knowledge of the Shaltus-controlled spellstone. Your half-brother must have realized you'd reached us—he's called back the soldiers he's had out hunting you."

Leah took a long sip of the *dinuuci*. It went down

smoothly, without a bitter aftertaste, but the warm glow it produced was evidence of its potency. Then she returned to her seat, picked up the tunic she'd been working on, and started to hem it.

"What does the council say about the Shaltus-wraith?" she asked.

"The consensus is that no Sylvan would aid a wraith. Most members of the council believe that you were wrong about Trask being poisoned or that if he were, it was by some accident. They don't want to believe that any Sylvan could do such a thing."

"And you, what do you believe?" asked Leah, glancing at him from the corners of her eyes.

"I am not so sure."

Quinen rose and paced the room. He looked worried. He circled the room once and stopped in front of the table where Leah worked. Then he refilled his glass of *dinuuci* and quickly downed it. Abstractly watching Leah's fingers whip tight stitches in the cloth, he seemed to search for the right words.

"I don't trust Geraed. He hates humans almost as much as I do, but for different reasons. His father was a *Shuull* priest, and his father before that. He's a fanatic. He believes *Shuull* wants us to destroy all the humans and extend our forests everywhere."

"Isn't that what you want?" asked Leah. Her eyes met his for a moment; then he looked guiltily away.

"Maybe. But at what price? I think Geraed is willing to do anything to achieve his ends, even dealing with a wraith. Have you heard of the Expansionists?"

Leah shook her head.

"It is a sect of the *Shuull* priesthood that believes that it is the Sylvan destiny to replace the humans. Some of the Expansionists aided S'Shegan during the Great War in the hope that the humans would destroy each other."

"Geraed belongs to this sect?"

"He is their leader. I believe he may be secretly aiding the Shaltus-wraith for the same reasons. The Expansionists believe that by sowing dissension among the humans they can maneuver them into destroying themselves."

"And you think Geraed is responsible for poisoning Trask?"

"I believe that Geraed thought that he would be made chief at Trask's death. He did not think that I had enough support in the council. However, as it turned out, I was the one appointed to take Trask's place, not Geraed."

Leah frowned. "I still don't understand why he would want to kill my grandfather. If Geraed wanted to aid Shaltus secretly, what did it matter if the tribe officially remained neutral?"

"Perhaps Trask found out what Geraed had done. Or perhaps the Expansionists now want open war with the humans."

Leah put down her sewing and sighed deeply. "I don't know. It is just so hard to believe that a *Shuull* priest would try to kill the tribal chief. It's against all Sylvan law."

She felt suddenly tense and distressed. "Even if Geraed did kill Trask, he's not going to admit it. And if he or any Sylvan aided the Shaltus-wraith, that's just going to make my brother more certain that I was involved. How can I ever prove to him that I wasn't?"

All the fear and uncertainty she'd been suppressing for days welled up against the barriers she'd erected and began to flood over the top. The strain had taken its toll on her defenses. For the first time she felt the desperate loneliness and fear she'd been hiding from everyone, especially from herself.

Her eyes blurred with tears, but years of rejection had built many protective layers. She fought for self-control, and only a single tear managed to slip beneath her long lashes and roll slowly down her cheek.

Quinen reached forward and brushed the tear from her face. His fingertips gently moved down her cheek and softly traced her lips, chin, and neck. As his hand reached her shoulder, he bent forward and kissed her lightly on the cheek. His arms tightened around her and pulled her up to him, while his lips moved to hers.

Leah responded automatically as he kissed her hungrily. Her body tingled with a warmth that seemed to burn like both fire and ice.

She remembered when he had kissed her before, long ago, but it had not been like this. Now there was no fog of alcohol to cloud her senses. Nor had she felt similar passion when she'd exchanged furtive kisses with a human boy on a dare.

Now she felt her body responding in a way that she had only dreamed about—never really believing that anyone, human or Sylvan, would want her this much.

His embrace seemed to offer the reassurance and acceptance that she desperately needed.

As his hands touched her intimately, she felt a strange mixture of desire and panic.

"I've wanted you for so long," he whispered. His hands caressed her. "But I tried not to. Do you know how beautiful you are?" She felt a burning that was a glow and suddenly realized that she had wanted him without ever knowing it.

At the same time a part of her mind remained coldly aloof and analytical. Was she ready for this? Did she really want it?

She liked him, she wanted him, but there was a coldness in him, a bitterness, a thirst for vengeance. His hatred of humans was deep and consuming. And she was half-human, after all. He would never really trust her, and thus she could never completely trust him.

Yet her lips, her fingers, her body were reacting to him and demanding as much from him as he was from her.

For a moment a feeling of panic took precedence as his hands pulled at her tunic. Her mental doubts overcame her body's longing, and she tried to pull away. Then the continued pressure of his hands and lips on her body defeated her fears. She reached for him.

As she yielded to the passion, it pushed all thoughts from her mind. She was awash in a sea of sensations that caressed her, pounded her, and covered her, until she seemed to drown in the ecstasy.

Sunlight splashed across Leah's face. She squeezed her eyes shut and cuddled down into the covers, trying to force her way back into pleasant, half-remembered dreams. The brightness of day intruded. She could not escape the sun's glare or the reality that it brought.

Sighing, she opened her eyes to stare at Quinen, who lay asleep beside her. His boyish face looked like a child's, unlined and untroubled.

Yet it was the face of a stranger. Although she'd spent the night getting to know his body, she'd learned little about the man himself. Their lovemaking had been passionate and tender, but they'd hardly spoken.

She felt confused and angry at herself. She'd always tried to keep herself under control, her emotions tightly reined. It was disturbing to discover that she was vulnerable in an area she'd hardly even thought about and that her alienation and loneliness were countered by deep-seated needs and desires far stronger than she had realized.

How could she have let this happen?

As she studied Quinen she still felt desire. But now

her mind was filled with doubt and self-recrimination, for her suspicions had been aroused during the night.

It seemed to her that during their lovemaking her psychic as well as her physical senses had been stimulated. Whether it was some leakage from Quinen's mind, since he was a telepath, or some sort of empathic reaction on her part, although she was not a telepath, she had been psychically aware of Quinen. His mind had been tightly shielded against her, as though he feared her sensing anything, even his surface thoughts and emotions.

Nevertheless, at the height of their passion, his shield had slipped for a fraction of a second. She had felt his surprise at her inexperience.

She had also sensed a kind of loneliness in him that matched her own. Then his shield had slammed shut, but not before she sensed emotions behind the loneliness—bitterness, hatred, and guilt. And the guilt had something to do with Trask.

The touch was so brief that she almost thought she had imagined it. However, it was just tantalizing enough to rearouse her suspicions. After all, except for Quinen's story about the Expansionists, Leah had no real reason to suspect Geraed of poisoning Trask. On the other hand, Quinen's possible motives were obvious. If Trask died, Quinen would become chief; he'd be in a position to counteract Trask's policy of peace toward humans; he could perhaps even aid Shaltus openly, although he might find opposition to an alliance with a wraith even among those who wanted war with the humans. Moreover, Quinen had tried to prevent her from helping Trask.

She tried to sort things our dispassionately. She had to accept what had happened between Quinen and herself without guilt or remorse. It had been an act of physical passion, nothing more.

After all, she told herself, the Sylvan approved of

promiscuity, and even the humans with their stricter
morals accepted sexual experimentation before marriage. Since she was a product of both cultures, she
should have no reason for moral misgivings. Actually
she should be pleased that it had happened, even
grateful, for it was long overdue.

As she brooded she decided that she was glad that
it had happened, at least from a physical and an
intellectual viewpoint; emotionally she was still not
quite certain.

It had become imperative for her to find out the
truth. She had to learn if Quinen was allied with the
Shaltus-wraith or if he had been correct in accusing
Geraed.

Realizing that her mental shield had slipped slightly during the night, she reinforced her barriers against
any telepathic probes. She had to be on her guard.
Fortunately she could shield herself as well as any
full-blooded Sylvan.

There had to be some spell, some sorcery that could
help her discover the truth. Distractedly clutching her
spellstone in her hand, she searched her knowledge
for an answer.

The only thing that occurred to her was a method
for eavesdropping. Since the Sylvan powers differed
greatly from human sorcery, she doubted that they
would be able to detect such a spell. She would need
to prepare an object and inscribe it with a rune. While
Quinen slept, she had a perfect chance to act.

Slipping quietly from the bed, she studied Quinen.
He remained soundly asleep. She felt the urge to
touch his brow, to kiss him gently into wakefulness
and desire, to feel his body against hers once more.

No! She had to keep in control of herself. She had
to take advantage of the present opportunity. There
was no way to know whether it would ever come
again.

She tiptoed over to his hastily discarded garments, picked up his knife belt, and retreated into the bathroom.

Pressing the edge of her spellstone against the back of the belt, she drew runes as she recited an incantation. This left a faint impression of lines on the leather. Then she rubbed the stone across the runes three times to impress the spell upon the object and to remove visible signs of the runes.

Finally she restored the belt to the pile of Quinen's clothes. Since he was still asleep, Leah chose some garments for herself and returned to the bathroom to shower and dress. She also wanted privacy to cast another spell, this one on herself.

She had to make certain that she would not bear Quinen's child.

When she finished she returned to find Quinen awake and dressing. Although her face betrayed no emotion, she tensed as he donned the knife belt, but he did not detect her magic.

Then he noticed her and said, "There's a council meeting this morning." He looked away, avoiding her gaze. "I have to hurry."

His manner was cool, almost brusque. At first Leah thought he was merely embarrassed; then as she watched his expression she began to wonder if he were actually angry with himself for what had happened. After all, she was a *shiffem*. In the clear light of day the fact that she was only a half-breed was all too obvious.

Not knowing what to say to him, she turned away, picked up her hairbrush from the table, and began to brush her waist-length, silver hair. Although her face remained impassive as she plaited it into a long Sylvan-style rope down the right side of her neck, her mind whirled with conflicting emotions of hurt, resentment, disappointment, anger, and longing.

"I'll see you later," said Quinen behind her. She glanced through the open bathroom door and caught sight of him reflected in the large oval mirror hanging over the sink. His expression was one of tenderness. Yet as she turned toward him, his face became colder. His eyes were tormented with doubt. Somehow she knew he hated himself for the feelings he had toward her, and he hated her for being half-human. Yet while he reproached himself for what had happened, she knew that he still wanted her.

"Later," he said, striding out of the room. The hesitation in his voice made the word a hollow promise.

Tightlipped, she watched the door close soundly behind him. She had to get herself under control. Until she could discover Quinen's role in the events of the past week, she could not afford any emotional involvement.

Sinking into a chair, she pulled out her spellstone and studied its amber depths. Slowly her rapport with the stone forced her mind into a calm, clear state.

She meditated for over an hour, until a serving boy arrived with her breakfast. The interruption brought her back to reality.

Although she remained disturbed by what had happened, the meditation had ordered the chaos of her thoughts and restored her equilibrium.

First she would eat, then test the runespell she'd imprinted on Quinen's belt; next she would try to enter Geraed's room to hide a similar rune there; finally she would visit her grandfather to see if he had improved.

She was going to discover the truth somehow.

Seven

After eating a hurried meal of fried *delaap* and *to-maad*, Leah cleared the table and placed the tray outside her door so that she wouldn't be disturbed. Then she removed the mirror from the bathroom and placed it flat on the table. The glass was a thirty-centimeter-wide oval.

As she concentrated on her spellstone and chanted, the mirror's surface clouded. She used her stone to redraw the runes on the surface of the mirror. Although the gem did not cut the glass, the lines of the glyphs remained as though they had been etched.

She continued the incantation while focusing her thoughts upon Quinen, his belt, and the runes inscribed on it. At the same time she slowly passed her stone over the surface of the mirror three times. The runes disappeared.

Placing the spellstone to her forehead, she stared at the mirror. Almost immediately it cleared, and Leah found herself looking at the front of Quinen's belt.

With careful control she shifted her viewpoint, pulling up and away from the belt until the image seemed to be from a vantage point a meter above and behind the top of Quinen's head.

He was sitting at a mirrored dressing table in his room, applying his face paint.

As Quinen drew a red semicircle on his left cheek,

Leah extended her visual range until she seemed to be watching from the farthest corner of the ceiling behind Quinen.

She tested her ability to hear within the room. Amplifying the sounds, she heard the tap of Quinen's fingers against the wooden makeup box, the whisper of the brush against his skin, the rasp of his breath, the thud of heartbeats. Then she reduced the level to about normal.

Quinen made no sign that he sensed her presence.

Satisfied that the magic was working, Leah was about to break off touch with the runespell when someone knocked on the door.

Quinen called, "Come in."

In walked a gaunt Sylvan with a short crimson line across his forehead and a design of blue and red on his right cheek. His face looked familiar, but it took Leah a moment to remember his name—Pazolt. He was a *Shuull* priest, subordinate to Geraed. Leah recalled that her grandfather had mentioned that the two priests did not get along well.

Curious, Leah stayed to watch. She felt uneasy. She didn't enjoy eavesdropping, but she had no choice.

Looking into his mirror at Pazolt's reflection, Quinen continued to apply his makeup.

"What is it?" he asked impatiently.

"I've just gotten word from the Expansionists in the Anoke forest. They've kidnapped Lady Barbara S'Carlton and are taking her to Bluefield."

"What's this?" Quinen swung around to face the priest.

"Evidently Lord S'Carlton was sending her to Richmond for safety. When our man learned about it they intercepted her party and captured her."

"Good. That's one less S'Carlton to worry about.

The wraith will be pleased—it wants to execute the S'Carltons itself, if possible, to sweeten its revenge."

The image in Leah's mirror wavered and began to cloud as she fought to control the anger and hurt that threatened to dissolve her rapport. She shuddered. So Quinen was allied to the Shaltus-wraith.

Taking a deep breath, she steadied her thoughts. She had to remain a detached observer. Strong emotions would break her concentration.

Resolutely she fixed her gaze on the mirror and reestablished contact with the runespell. The glass cleared.

". . . the sorcerer Rowen is planning to set out for Bluefield two days from now to attempt to destroy the Shaltus-wraith," said Pazolt. "We must send men to intercept him. We should be able to head him off and stage an ambush where the Bluefield Road passes along Ravencliffe's ridge."

"Are you sure he'd take that road?"

"It's the shortest route from Castle Carlton to Bluefield. He's bound to go that way."

Quinen nodded. Then he turned back to his makeup box and began painting a zigzag design of blue and purple across his right cheek as he talked.

"I'm going to dispose of him myself. I'll take a few men and leave after the council meeting. You'll remain here. I have to make certain that Rowen is eliminated. Shaltus thought that the programmed spellstone I planted among Leahdes's possessions would be strong enough to kill Richard S'Carlton and then wreck the castle. If it hadn't been for that blasted Rowen, I believe the wraith would have succeeded. He's a dangerous man. We can't afford to give him the chance to attack the wraith—he might be successful."

"Would that be so bad?" asked the priest. "I don't like aiding that wraith."

Quinen glanced up at him in the mirror and frowned. "Do you think I do? It's abhorrent. But the best way to conquer the humans is to allow them to destroy themselves. Ever since the first spellstones were discovered some centuries ago, the human sorcerers have engaged one another in a series of destructive wars, each one more devastating than the last. Occasionally we've managed to aid one side or the other, to the detriment of the whole. We helped S'Shegan during the Great War, until he became a bit too ambitious and attacked some of our forests. Helping the Shaltus-wraith is just one more step in the process. He'll be our tool to destroy the kingdom of Carlton without endangering ourselves."

"But if the wraith succeeds, can we be sure it will pose no threat to us?"

"A wraith has one goal; when it has been reached, the phantom will cease to exist. In this case Shaltus wants only revenge—the death of the S'Carlton family. When the last dies, so will the wraith."

Pazolt looked skeptical. "Can we be certain of that? Little is known of wraiths, and Shaltus is very powerful."

Quinen shrugged, but his odd-colored eyes looked worried. "We cannot be certain, of course, but from what we know of other wraiths we believe this to be the case. If it does not vanish, we will destroy it— we Sylvan have our powers too. In the meantime the wraith will work for us. It has promised that once Richard S'Carlton is dead it will destroy Castle Carlton and all the humans inside. We'll take over the kingdom, and in time our forest land shall increase a hundredfold."

There was a sudden pounding on the door. It swung open before Quinen could answer.

"Sorry to interrupt," said the Sylvan who entered. "I've urgent news. Trask is dead."

Fear and sorrow flickered across Leah's thoughts, but she kept her emotions tightly reined. The image in the glass never wavered.

The pain in Quinen's eyes seemed genuine. "This is a sad day," he said to the messenger. "Inform the other council members, please."

The man nodded and hurried from the room.

Lowering his brush, Quinen swiveled toward Pazolt.

"It had to be done." Quinen's voice was almost a sob. He slammed his fist into his palm. Then he pressed his hands against his forehead. "Damn it. Damn."

"It had to be done," echoed the priest with the hardness of steel.

"If only he hadn't found out that I was an Expansionist," muttered Quinen.

"Things will be easier for us now that you are chief," said Pazolt.

Quinen's shoulders straightened. He looked sad, but resigned. "Yes. But we must continue to work in secret. Most Sylvan will not accept any sort of pact with a wraith; even some of my own men would object. And there are those who supported Trask—they will still want peace with the humans. However, they can have no complaints if a wraith destroys Carlton.

"I've already arranged to get another Shaltus-controlled spellstone from the wraith. When I learned that Rowen had destroyed the first stone I had planted at Carlton I sent my man Vargo to Bluestone for another. Vargo should be back in a day or two. After we've ambushed Rowen I'll arrange to smuggle the new programmed stone into Castle Carlton. Without Rowen's interference it will destroy Lord Richard S'Carlton, the castle itself, and the humans within. Then we'll have to keep our part of the bargain and kill any surviving S'Carltons. Richard's other sister, Laurie, is married to Lord S'Richmond, and Richard has sent his two children to her for safekeeping. Unfortunately the kingdom of Richmond is in the area protected from sorcery by the Triad spellstones. However, it shouldn't be too hard to arrange for their deaths. With all those of S'Carlton blood dead the Shaltus-wraith will vanish, its vengeance complete."

"What about Leahdes?" asked the *Shuull* priest.

Quinen's face tensed. "I don't know. She's part Sylvan."

"She's part human," countered the priest. "She's of the same blood as those who killed your family, remember that. She's of S'Carlton's blood. The wraith will want her death."

"It never mentioned her when we made our pact."

"She's of S'Carlton's blood," Pazolt insisted. "The wraith's vengeance won't be complete without her death. Besides, she's a sorceress—she could be dangerous. She knows about the poisoning and may suspect you. She may find out that you have joined the Expansionists."

Quinen tapped his fists together nervously. "Don't worry. I've fed her some misinformation, so she won't suspect me. I've told her about the Expansionists, but I said that I opposed them. I told her that Geraed is the leader."

"Geraed!" Pazolt laughed heartily. "That's misdirection all right, naming one of Trask's major supporters as the head of the Expansionists."

"We know he opposes us, but she doesn't," Quinen replied.

Suddenly the humor was gone from Pazolt's smile. "But she could find out."

"I suppose so," Quinen admitted.

"She must die," said the priest.

Watching them, Leah felt her chest tighten in distress.

"No!" Quinen exclaimed.

The priest studied Quinen's troubled eyes. "You like her, don't you?"

Quinen shrugged and looked away.

"But that didn't stop you from planting the wraith's spellstone among her things. She could have died then."

"I know, but . . ."

"But you were with her last night."

"How . . ."

The priest smiled grimly. "I was looking for you. Someone said they'd seen you go into her room. She is a beautiful woman . . . but she is a human, not a Sylvan. She's lived with them, she knows their ways, she uses their magic. She is dangerous. She must die now, before she learns of our pact with Shaltus."

Quinen nodded reluctantly. His eyes were downcast, troubled with guilt.

"We'll make it look like a suicide," the priest continued. "Let her grieve over Trask's death. Then, upset by her grandfather's passing and her brother's accusations, Leahdes Carlton will take poison. We'll use something far less exotic than the drug we used on Trask. Hers will be a quick, painless death."

"I don't like doing it," said Quinen, raising his eyes for a moment to look almost defiantly at Pazolt. Then he looked away and stared into space. "You are right. I can see that it is necessary. And the tribe will believe a suicide." His face hardened but the pain lingered in his eyes. "Do it while I'm away."

"Of course."

Suddenly Leah could no longer suppress her anger and despair. As her control dissolved, the image in the mirror vanished. The runespell was broken.

Seeing herself now reflected in the glass, she picked

up the mirror and smashed it against the table. As it shattered, a shard cut into her palm.

The pain was like a rocky promontory, solid and real. She held on to it against the force of the emotions that stormed her mind—anger, fear, grief, desolation, and despair. The reality of the pain focused the torment of her feelings into a wedge of desperation.

I have to get out of here, she thought, staring at her hand. *I've got to.*

She removed the shard of glass and bandaged her hand with a piece of *dolaan* torn from one of the garments she'd been altering. Then she changed into trousers and a short tunic and put on her boots.

The pain was becoming a numbness echoing in her mind. She felt dazed and suddenly uncertain. She jabbed her fingernails into the bandaged cut deliberately. The pain stabbed through her hand, shot up her arm, and cut away the fog enveloping her thoughts. She had to concentrate on it and use it to block the emotions that threatened to paralyze her.

She had to escape.

As she glanced around the room for a final time, she saw herself reflected in one of the pieces of broken glass. Her face had an unnatural harshness. Her jaw was clenched, her lips were tight and flat, her odd-colored eyes were as cold as ice. Taking a deep breath, she forced her features to relax. She had to look normal. After a moment her face became an emotionless mask, marred only by the slight trace of frost lingering in her gaze.

Taut and tense, she drew another deep breath. Then looking as though nothing had happened, she strolled toward the door. But as she was about to open it, someone knocked urgently on the other side.

Startled, she jerked away. She gripped her spellstone tightly in her injured hand. Its polished surface was warm to the touch. Her fingers pressed against it seeking strength in its power. Then she opened the door.

It was Geraed.

Leah's tension eased only a fraction as she bade him enter.

The *Shuull* priest looked troubled.

"I have some sad news," he said, pulling the door shut behind him. "Trask is dead."

Leah sighed. "I know."

"You've heard?" Geraed seemed surprised.

Leah nodded. She shouldn't have blurted that out. Now Geraed was glancing curiously at the smashed mirror on the table. What was she going to tell him?

She tried to remember what Pazolt had said about his superior—something about Geraed being one of Trask's supporters. He was opposed to the Expansionists. Yet could she really trust him? She felt as though she were walking through a swamp with every path leading into quicksand.

"I sent a message over to Quinen," the priest continued. "I thought I ought to tell you myself. You did your best for your grandfather, but I'm afraid your human magic was no better than Sylvan powers."

He glanced again at the broken glass. He started to speak, then decided against it. Clearing his throat, he backed toward the door. "I'd better go now. I have to make the preparations for Trask's funeral. It will be tomorrow at sunset."

As he began to turn away, Leah suddenly called him back. "Geraed . . ." She hesitated, still uncertain of him but knowing that this would be her last chance to gain his help.

"Yes?" His mismatched eyes of copper and hazel studied her face with concern.

If she wanted to stop Quinen's plan from succeeding, she had to trust someone.

"I've found out that Quinen did poison Trask!"

"So? How do you know that?"

"I used the human magic you dislike so much to eavesdrop on him." She had made her choice.

Swiftly she outlined the conversation she'd heard between Quinen and Pazolt.

When she finished, Geraed nodded. He seemed surprised by some of the details, but not by the fact that Quinen had joined the Expansionists or that they had made an alliance with Shaltus.

"I knew that Pazolt was one of the Expansionists," he said. "But I wasn't sure that Quinen had joined them. This explains some things—like how Quinen got enough support in the council to become chief when Trask fell ill. Several council members are Expansionists."

"You've got to stop them," Leah exclaimed.

The Sylvan priest shook his head doubtfully. "I don't know that I can. You don't understand my position here—it's not very strong. Quinen knows I suspect him of poisoning Trask. He may move against me next. So I've got to act cautiously.

"I don't like humans very much, but I decided long ago that Trask was right to seek peace. That's why I supported him. The world is large enough for both groups. A war between the Sylvan and the humans would be devastating to both sides. Although the Expansionists think they can avoid war, every move they make brings us closer to it."

He seemed to be thinking aloud more than talking to her. "Perhaps they've gone too far now in dealing with a wraith to gain their ends. Even the Sylvan who want war with the humans would oppose such an alliance. If I can expose the pact they've made with Shaltus, perhaps I can stop them. But I've got to go slowly and carefully. I can't move yet. In the meantime, Leahdes, it's up to you to warn your brother. I'll do what I can here."

Leah shuddered, remembering the hatred she'd seen in her half-brother's eyes. "I don't know that he would believe me or even that he would give me the chance to explain what's happened. I don't think I dare return to Castle Carlton."

"But you must. You've got to prevent the ambush that Quinen plans for that sorcerer, Rowen—he may be the only man capable of destroying the Shaltus-wraith. The wraith could be as dangerous to us as to the humans. It must be eliminated. Right now there's nothing I can do to contact Rowen or Lord S'Carlton. You've got to warn them."

"Rowen . . ." mused Leah. "Perhaps I could talk to him. His friend helped me once; they might believe me. Then Lord Rowen could explain things to my half-brother. But I don't think that Richard would listen to me."

"Then that's what you must do." Geraed glanced at the door. "But you must leave quickly, now, before Quinen thinks to have you watched. Can you find your way to the stable?"

Leah nodded.

"You'd better go alone," said Geraed. "It would be best if they think I had no part in this. They'll wonder why you suddenly left the forest."

"By the time they realize that I must have stumbled across the truth, it will be too late for them to stop me." She studied Geraed's face, still wondering if she had been a fool to trust him. But what choice did she have? She smiled at him grimly. "Be careful."

"You also."

Then Leah took a deep breath, brought her features into a calm mask of indifference, and strolled out the door.

Passing Sylvan paid no attention to her as she descended a series of rope ladders and interior tree stairs, following a path to the forest floor that she remembered from past visits to Trask. As a *shiffem* she was beneath their notice.

When she reached the ground it took her only a few minutes to locate the great tree that was used as a stable. Its diameter was over twenty meters.

She approached cautiously. As she expected, there were no Sylvan guards outside. Sentries were stationed around the perimeter of the forest to stop unwarranted visitors from entering. There was no need to prevent anyone from leaving.

Still, she knew there would be a couple of Sylvan within the stable. Although she could probably get a horse and ride away without arousing suspicion, she planned to take a pack horse, supplies, and a quantity of *tomaad*, and she had no way to explain those.

She inspected the tree and found the almost invisible outline of its large double doors. Cupping her powerstone in her hands, she recited a spell. Then she twisted the knobby protuberance of wood that served as the door handle.

The double doors, large enough for a horse and rider, swung open. The interior of the tree had been hollowed out into an enormous room with a dome ceiling. The living wood had been shaped to form stalls, saddle racks, storage shelves, even a hayloft over part of the room. Like all walls within the skytrees the barn's were covered with a dark brown moss that provided phosphorescent lighting.

Leah hesitated at the entrance and warily studied the interior.

Several Sylvan sat at a table in the front of the room. They had been playing a card game when her spell hit. Now they were frozen in their places. Their hands clutched oblong cards that their eyes no longer saw. They would remain suspended for about half an hour. When the spell lifted they would return to consciousness and would not even notice that any time had passed.

Leah used her spellstone to probe for signs of other Sylvan, but there were none.

She swiftly found her chestnut mare and saddled it. Then she chose a dark brown gelding from the back of the barn. Like other Sylvan horses it had been specially bred for its size. She packed it with a variety of supplies from the shelved stockpiles, including several small casks of *tomaad*, canteens of *tomaad* and water, journeycakes, some salted venison, and a small supply of *delaap* nuts. She didn't think that a casual inspection would reveal the small amount of missing goods.

As a *shiffem* Leah had one advantage over the Sylvan; she could live on *delaap* and *tomaad*, but they weren't essential parts of her diet. The perishable nature of the skytree nuts limited the length of time that the Sylvan could remain away from their forests.

When she finished she took the horses outside and closed the stable doors behind her.

For a moment her fingers clung to the rough bark of the skytree. She could sense its strength and serenity. She longed to reach out and mesh with it as she had with the oak. But she dared not take the time.

Reluctantly she pulled her hands away from the tree. She mounted and urged her horses forward. She had decided to try to intercept Lord Rowen before he reached Ravenscliffe.

Leah felt as though her emotions had been rubbed raw until she could feel nothing except a throbbing numbness. But through the numbness there was one spark of emotion still driving her.

She had come to the forest seeking refuge. She had almost dared hope that it would be more than that

—a home. But her sanctuary had become a death-trap. Now she was an exile, condemned by both worlds. Yet she could not flee. Though neither the Sylvan nor the humans wanted her, she was of them both. And she was as prideful as they.

Although she was without home or friends and should have had no duty to anyone except herself, the ties of her past chained her to responsibilities from which she could not free herself.

She had loved and respected her father, and she could not now see his kingdom and his family destroyed because of her inaction. Yet part of her would have been glad to do nothing to save Carlton and its lord.

She had also loved and respected her grandfather. She felt duty-bound to save his dream of peace between Sylvan and human, if she could.

Yet the part of her that had been hurt and rejected by both sides almost wanted to see their destruction.

But her pride held her to her duty, and she had no choice in what she must do.

Eight

Leah had no difficulty leaving the Sylvan forest. Throughout the long day she followed the Twelve-people River southeastward on the rough, deserted trail. The summer sun beat relentlessly against the forest, keeping the air stifling hot, despite the shade. As the miles passed, the river dwindled into a stream and then a creek, while the trees pressed in on the trail and threatened to swallow it altogether at every turn and dip.

The afternoon shadows became elongated black spears cutting through the dusk-darkened trail. A cool breeze finally began to flow along the narrow pathway. Although it was refreshing, the sudden change of temperature made Leah shiver.

The wind tasted of moisture, leaves, and night, but there was something more—smoke up ahead. She had almost reached the fork in the trail that would head east to the Bluefield Road, where she'd planned to camp.

Leah sniffed the air again. It smelled of burning wood, roasting nuts, and frying fish. Someone must be camped at the fork.

Slowing her horse, she wondered who would be traveling the out-of-the-way trail. A hunter perhaps? A Sylvan traveling from Anoke to Ayers or vice versa? Or perhaps some soldiers still looking for her?

The smoke was nearer. She dismounted and led her

horses forward cautiously. Her fingers nervously
rubbed the surface of her spellstone. She could have
used it to sense what lay ahead, but any sorcerer
would then be alerted to her presence.

The smell of frying fish made her mouth water. She
was very close.

Dropping the horses' reins, she crept forward until
she reached the edge of the clearing where the trail
forked. She pressed her body against a thick tree
trunk, trying to make herself a part of the deep
shadows and the wood.

A lone Sylvan sat at a campfire in the center of the
glade. He was a member of the Ayers tribe, but Leah
couldn't remember his name.

She wondered if she dare step forward and claim
traveler's rights. It was common practice for way-
farers to extend hospitality to one another. That fish
looked tempting. Probably the Sylvan had been
traveling for some distance and was running low on
supplies of *delaap* nuts, or he wouldn't eat fish. It was
becoming too dark for her to travel farther anyway.
The campfire looked very inviting.

But if this were one of Quinen's men, he could have
been in telepathic contact with the new Sylvan chief
and warned to watch for her.

She decided that she could not risk a meeting. As
she began to ease backward, the Sylvan turned in
her direction. She froze. He was not looking at her.
It seemed as if he'd just remembered something he
should do. He rose and walked to his saddlebag. He
removed a small pouch from one of the side packets.

When his fingers reached into the bag, his head
tilted. The firelight clearly illuminated his features.

In that moment Leah remembered the man's
name, Vargo. She realized with dreadful certainty
that the pouch contained the Shaltus-programmed

spellstone that Quinen had sent for. The Sylvan's fingers touched the wraithstone. It came alive.

This stone had evidently been structured with more of Shaltus's personality than the crystal planted at Carlton, for there was no mistaking the origin of the dark well of force that Leah sensed. It was powerful, dangerous, malignant.

At its touch Leah reacted automatically, without thinking. Her spellstone flared blue-white, and a golden aura of protective force enveloped her.

Instantly she knew her mistake, but it was too late. The Shaltus-stone had not been aware of her presence until she had used her power. If she had not acted, it might never have sensed her. Now it probed toward her, touched her shield, and somehow recognized her.

A blast of force slammed into her. As it met her shield flares of intense light bounced off of it. A corona of silver and gold enveloped her. Fire scorched her skin but did not burn it. Thunder blasted her eardrums. The air reeked of ozone and sulfur.

The attack broke off. She had withstood it easily.

She saw the Sylvan staring at her with surprise and fear. He glanced at the wraithstone which he still held. He looked ready to toss it away and run.

Suddenly Vargo's fingers clenched tightly around the stone. His head jerked back and forth. His features contorted. His legs and arms twitched frantically.

Then it was as if something snapped into place. His face and body became calm. But they were no longer Vargo's.

The features had subtly altered—the jawline was harder, the lips firmer, the skin tighter. The face was somehow handsomer, older, crueler.

The Shaltus-wraith possessed Vargo. Or rather the echo of the wraith did, for the personality impressed on the programmed stone was only a carbon copy of the wraith, as the wraith was only a shadow of the man, Shaltus. It was a wraith of a wraith.

The man who had been Vargo laughed. The roar was deep, sensuous, exultant, menacing—and totally unlike Vargo's laugh.

As he laughed, Leah counterattacked. The wraith-stone threw up a shimmering protective shield around the Sylvan. Streamers of crimson flame surrounded him as her spell hit, but she could not penetrate the barrier.

Suddenly the branches of the trees on each side of Leah stirred and flowed unnaturally. The wraith was using Vargo's Sylvan powers.

Bark-stiff arms grabbed her. Twigs became fingers that held her in an unbreakable vise. The wood had become as strong as steel.

Leah knew better than to use her human magic against the Sylvan power directly, for it would have had no effect, so she continued to blast Vargo with spells.

The tree whipped her through the air. The branches flung her toward the sky, smashed her against the ground, and tossed her upward again.

Her defensive shield absorbed most of the force of the blow, saving her from almost certain death at the impact. But the drubbing bruised her, made her nose bleed, and left her head ringing.

Then the limbs whirled her around and hurtled her toward the ground again. She screamed. At the last moment the branches twisted. Instead of hitting the ground she snapped up and down in the air. Finally the tree stilled.

She found herself hanging upside down closer to the edge of the clearing, only a couple of meters from Vargo.

Her sorcery had not touched him.

"No. That's too quick a death," he said. The voice

was deeper than Vargo's had been and held no trace of the lilting Sylvan accent.

"Too easy a death for one of S'Carlton blood."

Leah felt the branches tighten around her wrists and ankles. She struggled to free herself, but the boughs were as unyielding as bands of iron. They lifted her into a horizontal position and began to pull her in opposite directions.

"Your father put me on a rack . . ." Vargo chuckled. The sound of it was like fingernails grating against sandpaper.

Leah closed her eyes and tried to ignore the pain as the tree stretched her body as taut as a bowstring.

She murmured a spell. The branches of the tree began to flame.

The wraithstone reacted swiftly with a wind that extinguished the fire.

Leah changed the wind into a hurricane that tore violently at tree and Sylvan.

The hurricane became a tornado. It whirled into the sky and disappeared.

Leah felt as if her arms were being pulled from their sockets. She battered the wraith-protected Sylvan with several strong spells, but the stone countered each one.

The fear that had been with her since she had identified Vargo intensified and threatened to overwhelm her. Her powers and those of the wraith-controlled stone seemed equally matched, but the wraith would have the advantage as long as he used Vargo's Sylvan powers against her.

She doubted that Vargo was a very skilled shaper, for she'd never seen him wear the face paint that denoted high mastery of the craft. However, she knew that his Sylvan powers were still far superior to hers. Would it do any good to attack on that level?

Razor-edged pain cut across her thoughts as the

tree pulled a bit harder. The intervals between its movements were becoming longer. The shadow-wraith was savoring the torture.

She decided to try her Sylvan powers—another pull and she'd be screaming, the next and she wouldn't be able to concentrate enough for magic, after that she'd be unconscious or worse.

Focusing on her spellstone, she forced her mind into a calm, clear state. Then she melded with the tree.

She could sense the spirit of the wraith around her like a malignancy within the fiber of the wood. If it could sense her, it gave no sign.

She probed into the heart of the tree and felt its untouched core of strength. She sucked eagerly at the energy. It was invigorating.

Then she moved into the branches that held her body. She tried to shape the wood. Vargo's Sylvan powers were far stronger than hers, however. She could not move the boughs.

So she tried tapping the tree's strength within the branches.

Instantly there was a change.

The Shaltus-wraith was pouring energy into the tree to shape it, and Leah found herself absorbing that energy. The faster she took the power, the faster the wraith had to channel it in to maintain its control of the tree.

The flux of energy flowed around and through her in an exhilarating tide. It happened far too quickly for the wraith to sort through Vargo's mind for a means to stop it.

Leah was getting stronger; Vargo was weakening.

Suddenly a spasm shook the tree as the Sylvan lost control. The branches relaxed into normalcy.

Leah fell, rolled, and pulled herself erect. Severing

her contact with the tree, she focused all her energy into her shield.

As she turned toward Vargo and saw the Sylvan collapse, the wraithstone struck at her. The air around her flared with white-hot flame.

She countered it easily and blasted the Shaltus-programmed stone. She could sense that there was no longer any danger from the Sylvan. The wraith-stone had drained him of strength in its attempt to continue the torture. Vargo was dead.

The wraithstone glowed yellow, then orange, then red, as she continued her assault. Its energy stores were greatly depleted. It could no longer attack her.

The stone turned blue and purple-violet as she transformed the energy she'd taken from it into a weapon against it. Its colors deepened into brown and gray-black.

It exploded. A white fireball flung Leah back against the ground. Its glare blinded her.

During the battle she'd been able to ignore the pain of the torture. Now it was a sudden throbbing agony that made her cry out.

She lay there, not wanting to move, almost not wanting to live. But as she blinked her sight came back, and she found herself staring at the dead black lump that had been the wraithstone.

I've got to destroy it completely, she thought.

The air smelled of ozone, fire, and fish. The latter made her mouth water. She smiled inwardly at the absurdity of feeling hunger while she felt so much pain. Glancing at the fire, she saw a pan of fried trout and a few skytree nuts on the ground, waiting to be eaten. Nearby sat a jug. *Tomaad* had to be in that jug.

Her legs and arms didn't want to move. They felt like rubber that had been pulled too far and could no longer snap back.

Easing herself up on hands and knees, she pushed herself erect. She lurched forward and staggered past Vargo's body to the fire. Clumsily picking up the jug, she took several long sips of the *tomaad*.

The Sylvan elixir quickly eased her pain and restored her strength. After some minutes she felt well enough to examine the wraithstone.

Although it was blackened, cracked, and apparently harmless, she approached it cautiously. The aura of her shield glimmered with reflected firelight. She did not sense the Shaltus-wraith, and it did not react to her presence.

Taking a deep breath, she picked up the stone. The sun had now set and the glade was dim, so she had to bring it close to the fire to see it clearly. It was about the size of a small gold coin. One side had a jagged edge. Obviously it was only a broken piece of a larger spellstone.

She wondered where Shaltus had gotten a supply of powerstones. They were extremely rare. He would not have broken his original stone into pieces even for his revenge, for that would have greatly lessened, if not destroyed, his power.

As she stared at the crystal, she suddenly knew its origin. Both this stone and the one planted at Carlton had once been part of a larger spellstone—her father's.

She and her half-brother had been with her father when he'd tried to destroy the Shaltus-wraith. They'd stayed behind, about four kilometers from the Shaltus spellstone, while their father had gone in, believing the stone could be destroyed only at close range. They were to watch and learn from his mistakes, if he failed.

He'd never come out. And they hadn't had the power to go far enough into the Shaltus-controlled area to retrieve his body.

Evidently the wraith had taken her father's spell-stone and had broken it into several pieces. Then he'd programmed the fragments with his own personality and thirst for vengeance. Since the stone had been in the S'Carlton family for generations, it would have been somewhat attuned to those of S'Carlton blood, and thus it would be the perfect tool to use against them.

The piece of crystal was dead now, but Leah wanted to take no chances. She pressed it against her own stone and blasted it with magic. The wraithstone crumbled into ash that scattered on the wind.

She sighed with relief. She had won this time, but she had no doubt that the outcome would have been different if she had met the actual Shaltus-wraith, which was far more powerful.

Leah took a deep breath of air. It was moist and cool, and the acrid smells of sorcery were almost gone. The aroma of the cooked trout was strong and invit-ing.

Oh, well, she thought, sinking to her knees next to the fire. *There's no use wasting good food.* She laughed. Her body shuddered and tingled with the sudden release of tension.

She picked up the almost cool trout and took a hearty bite.

Nine

The next day Leah took the left fork in the trail. It cut almost due east through woods and farmlands and intersected the Bluefield Road a few miles south of Iveysville. The road had been wide enough for large wagons and coaches when it had been the main thoroughfare between the castles of Carlton and Bluefield. But now that Shaltus controlled Bluefield it was rarely used south of Iveysville and was in poor repair. Weeds and brush broke through the gravel surface. Even a few saplings were beginning to take hold. The only clear area was a rough track on the right, just wide enough for a single horseman.

At this point the road ran alongside a creek, so Leah camped on its bank. She was far enough away from the road to be unobtrusive, but close enough to watch it.

She waited for two days, growing more anxious with each hour that passed. Finally the whisper of hooves became drumbeats that shattered the forest's peace.

Leah slipped from her concealed campsite to the side of the road. She watched approaching patches of color coalesce into the forms of five riders—Rowen, Rusty, Fletcher, and two of S'Carlton's men.

She stepped onto the road.

As they caught sight of her the men halted. All except Rusty seemed startled to see her. The precog's pale big eyes held no surprise, only worry.

"N'Omb's fires!" exclaimed Fletcher.

Michael Rowen dismounted. The others followed. "We heard you were with the Sylvan," he said.

Leah nodded. She felt tense and afraid, not knowing what Rowen thought of her. "I went there to discover whether they had planted the programmed spellstone at Carlton."

Rowen was silent. His keen eyes looked thoughtful, but not hostile.

Rusty smiled shyly at her, as though he were glad to find her alive. "I thought you might show up before we reached Bluefield, but I wasn't sure. Sometimes I have flashes of foresight, whether I want them or not. But the future has many alternate paths. Without proper control I see only a jumble and don't know which is the most probable." He sighed. "Anyway, what did you find out from the Sylvan?"

"One of the Sylvan had hidden the spellstone among my things," Leah explained. "His name is Quinen. He's part of a sect called the Expansionists that wants to destroy humans and take over their lands. The Expansionists have formed an alliance with the Shaltus-wraith. Even now they are moving to ambush you, up the road at Ravenscliffe. With you dead they planned to smuggle another programmed spellstone into the castle to kill my half-brother. Quinen had sent for a new stone, but I chanced upon it on my way here and managed to destroy it."

"Then you came here to warn us?" asked Rusty.

"Yes." Leah sighed. "I dared not go back to Carlton to tell my brother. I thought perhaps you could warn him, convince him . . ."

"How do we know you're telling us the truth?" interrupted one of the soldiers. He was one of Richard S'Carlton's lieutenants, a man named Klaus. "This

Quinen you speak of couldn't be doing anything without the Sylvan chief's approval, and that means your grandfather."

"Trask is dead," said Leah. She told them of Quinen's treachery and of Geraed's offer to help. Her voice was flat as she recited the events. She felt emotionally drained.

"Then most of the Sylvan don't know of the pact with Shaltus?" asked Rowen when she'd finished.

"No. They wouldn't approve if they did. Even those who want war with the humans would find the idea of an alliance with a wraith repugnant. And there are many who don't want war. If Geraed can expose the pact that the Expansionists have made with the wraith, it might destroy the sect's power."

Obviously still skeptical, Lieutenant Klaus shook his head. "Lord S'Carlton said that she's a traitor. He ordered her execution. I don't doubt that part of her story is true, all right—the part about the alliance between the Sylvan and the wraith. But she's a Sylvie too, and she's going to lead us right into a trap. . . ."

"I don't think so." Rowen's deep voice cut into Klaus's words with the edge of command. "But there is one way to make certain."

Dropping his horse's reins, he stepped forward to face Leah. "Give me your spellstone."

Leah studied his face. His handsome features were unyielding; his eyes were cold steel.

Fear stabbed through her like a knife. She did not know this man; yet she had gambled her life in coming to him. Now he wanted her only protection. Once it was more than a hand's length from her body, she would not be able to control the spellstone. Gripping the stone tightly in her right hand, she hesitated. Then she realized that in coming here she'd already decided to trust him. She pulled the amulet over her head and gave it to Lord Rowen.

He tucked the chain casually into his belt and pulled his own stone forward. The amethyst crystal glowed with pale white light.

Leah tensed as he stepped toward her. She half-expected to feel an attack. Instead Rowen placed his crystal against the center of her forehead. It was flesh-warm.

Glancing back to the others, Rowen announced, "A truthspell shall give us the answer."

Leah's tension drained away. She knew that such spells were possible, but she'd never seen one used. She'd heard they were difficult to master and required intense concentration.

"A lie will turn the stone red; the truth will keep it white," said Rowen. He murmured a long incantation. His stone brightened into a steady white flame.

Then he questioned her about her visit to the sky-tree forest.

As she repeated the story of what happened, she left out only her affair with Quinen. It wasn't pertinent, and it embarrassed her. Rowen's spellstone remained bathed in silver light, confirming her veracity.

"All right," exclaimed Klaus finally. He frowned. Although he didn't like sorcery, he had lived under the rule of sorcerers all his life, so he accepted its use and reliability. Also, he knew Rowen's reputation. If such a sorcerer's powers deemed Leah's story to be the truth, he had to believe it.

The inner light vanished from Rowen's stone as he let it fall back against his chest. He returned Leah's stone. She felt a lot more secure when she'd put it back around her neck.

Suddenly she remembered something that she had forgotten to tell them. She frowned.

"There's something else. I also overheard Pazolt tell Quinen that the Expansionists have kidnapped my half-sister Barbara."

"But she was sent to Richmond for safety . . ." interjected Fletcher.

"Evidently some of the Expansionists in the Anoke forest intercepted her and are taking her to Bluefield. Shaltus seems to want to eliminate the S'Carltons by his own hand, if possible."

Rowen slammed his fist into his palm. "I'm the one who suggested that Barbara go to Richmond. It took her only a day to recover from the backlash of the wraith's attack, but I thought she'd be safer in the area controlled by the Triad. She left six days ago—no, seven."

Leah's eyes widened. She felt a sudden surge of hope. "Do you have a map of the area? I don't think they could have taken her all the way to Bluefield yet."

"I have a good one," replied Tim Fletcher. The thin, bearded man turned to his horse, opened one of his saddlebags, and pulled out a bundle of documents. Leah caught sight of a leather-bound book among the papers. She couldn't be sure, but it looked like a copy of The Book of Revelations, the sacred scriptures of N'Omb. Although the local Church had discouraged her father from bringing her to services, he had taught her its basic tenets. She knew that only members of the priesthood were permitted to read the sacred text. It was written in an ancient language, said to be the foundation for their present tongue, and only the N'Omb priests were taught its use. A greatly bowdlerized and reworked version of The Book of Revelations, called the Testaments of N'Omb, was available in the common language.

Before Leah could be certain of what she'd seen Fletcher had thrust the book back into his bag, along with most of the other documents. He sorted through several rolled maps and handed one to Rowen.

Leah knelt beside the tall sorcerer as he spread the

map on the ground. She studied the jagged line representing the Apple Mountains, which headed through the bottom third of Carlton northeast to the middle of the kingdom of Westvirn on Carlton's eastern border. To the south of the mountains lay the smaller, triangular-shaped state of Richmond.

To reach Castle Richmond on the coast, Barbara would undoubtedly have traveled along the lengthy St. Topher Road, which ran from Castle Carlton all the way through Westvirn to Castle Richmond. The highway crossed the mountains by way of the Clearfield Gap, quite close to the large Sylvan forest of Anoke.

It seemed likely that the Expansionists from the Anoke tribe had waylaid Barbara somewhere east of the Gap. They probably would have taken her back through the Gap and then headed south along the Greenstone and Bluestone rivers to Bluefield, rather than travel back to Anoke, where other Sylvan would have asked questions. The Expansionists had to be only a small minority of the Anoke tribe.

With the mountains to slow them the Sylvan could not have reached Bluefield yet. They were probably traveling southwest along the Greenstone River now.

Leah outlined her deductions to the others.

Rowen nodded. "We might be able to cut southeast along this trail." His finger stabbed at the map, pointing out a rough track that veered away from the main Bluefield Road just south of Iveysville, not far from their present position. It followed the left branch of the creek around the area known as Coal Mountain, while the main road followed the right branch and then angled south along Ravenscliffe Ridge.

"We could intercept them somewhere along the Bluestone River just before they enter the area that Shaltus controls." Rowen stood and looked thoughtfully at Rusty. "You might be able to help."

The stocky precog shook his head. "No."

Sighing, Rowen half-turned away from the older man. "Of course if you don't mind Lady S'Carlton's death on your conscience . . ." He shrugged.

"Damn it, Michael," exclaimed Rusty. "That's not fair. You know how I feel about seeing what's ahead." His fingers tugged restlessly at the end of the once russet-colored beard that had given him his nickname. It was almost all white now.

His too-wise eyes were seas of sadness. Then he nodded reluctantly. "All right. I guess we might as well find out what we're up against, if we can. But I'm not guaranteeing anything."

Klaus and the other soldier looked bewildered. They hadn't realized that Rusty was a precog.

Rusty pulled a half-empty bottle of brandy from his saddle and took a long swig. Fletcher grabbed his arm as the older man started to take a second drink.

"That's enough."

The anger in the precog's eyes faded. "Sure." He handed Fletcher the bottle. Then his eyes seemed to focus somewhere in midair. His face beaded with sweat, and deep lines etched his brow. His eyes began to roll up until mostly white showed. His face seemed to age ten years in a few seconds.

Leah sucked in her breath.

As the seconds ticked by with dreadful slowness, Lord Rowen looked plainly worried, and Fletcher seemed concerned. The soldiers were startled and confused by Rusty's sudden trance. Klaus hastily drew a circle in midair to signify a prayer to N'Omb.

Rusty's eyes snapped open. Fletcher put a supporting arm around his shoulders. The precog pulled the brandy from Fletcher's grip and took several long gulps. He sighed, pushed the bottle away from his lips, and raised his eyes to lock them with Rowen's.

"Well, Leah seems to be right. There's a chance we can catch up with Lady Barbara before she reaches Shaltus. However, it might be better if we don't try to save her."

"Why not?" asked Leah.

Rusty looked at her sadly. "The future is like a spider's web, with many strands. You can choose which to go down if you know the pattern. Instead of reaching the spider you were destined for you might reach the edge and safety." He glanced meaningfully at Michael Rowen. "Or you might fall off."

"What sort of magic have you done?" asked Klaus with hesitation. He was curious, but it was difficult for him to overcome his fear of sorcery.

"Rusty has the ability to foresee the future," replied Lord Rowen. "It requires no spellstone."

"Well, what have you seen?" Klaus asked Rusty.

"It's not easy to explain. I see a pattern of events. Those that are closest in time to the present are the clearest, those farther away are faint and unreadable. Within the pattern the details are sharpest on the most likely line of the future; but with each possible decision the path branches, and these alternate futures soon grow too numerous to trace. Sometimes there are swirls of lines around certain key events or people. Sometimes I can see these nodes clearly and discover the general future if certain things happen, or if they don't. Of course, the events that are the easiest to see are those that involve me. They are in the center of the general pattern."

Rusty took a long sip of the brandy. "There was a time in my life when I could study the paths for hours. I could follow the branches outward and outward until I thought I could predict just about anything." His face grew sadder. "But I was wrong. I couldn't trace out all the effects of a decision. One action can reverberate forever. . . ."

The precog shook his head as if trying to shake himself loose from some bitter memory. "Now, of course, I'm out of shape for such fine viewing. Even when I haven't had a drink, I can't concentrate for more than a few minutes. And I really don't want to." He glared at Lord Rowen. "I shouldn't be trying to read the future at all.

"So what I advise is probably worth nothing. I saw a chance that we might arrive at the Bluestone River in time to save Lady Barbara. But there's a greater chance they'll travel a little faster, and we'll miss them. Even if we do get there and don't get ourselves killed, those Sylvan that Miss Leah told us about, the ones waiting at Ravenscliffe, would probably learn what we've done and come after us. Then we'd have them to worry about."

"But if there is a chance to save Lady Barbara, we must take it!" interjected Lieutenant Klaus. "Lord S'Carlton would demand it. And he is the one paying for your services."

"I think Klaus has a point," replied Lord Rowen. "And I wouldn't feel right if we didn't at least try to save Lady Barbara."

"We'd be putting ourselves in a great deal of danger. . . ." Rusty insisted.

"What sort of danger?" asked Klaus. "You see what's ahead. Why can't you direct us away from any hazards?"

Rusty's fists clenched. "You don't understand. I just get glimpses now. Sometimes it's as though I were standing on a mountain, looking down at a river—I can see that the current is swift and dangerous, but I can't chart every rock in the rapids. I can't tell if those dark objects in the water are logs, rocks, or gators. I know that there is a way down the river. If you are on a sturdy raft and have luck and skill, you might make it. However, I have enough sense to know that only a fool would try it."

He frowned, searching for the right words. "Sometimes my vision is full of detail. It's as if I'm down on that raft, and I know every rock and current ahead. Yet at the same time I'm so close to the river that I can just get a glimpse of the mountain. I don't know what's on the mountainside or beyond it. From that vantage point I don't know where the river will lead or even what's beyond the next bend."

"But you do see a chance to rescue Lady Barbara?" asked Klaus impatiently.

"Yes. I see a path that leads to her. But that way holds dangers for each of us." With his last words Rusty gestured toward the rest of the group. The expression on his face seemed to indicate that he'd envisioned a death for everyone in the party in at least one possible future.

Leah shivered as she realized that Rusty had included her in the group. What made him think that she was going along? She hadn't thought about anything beyond warning Rowen of Quinen's plans. She didn't know what she was going to do next, but it hadn't even entered her mind that she might accompany them to Bluefield.

She thought about the dangers lying in that direction—the deadly Shaltus-wraith waiting for another chance to destroy her, the Sylvan who were taking her half-sister to Shaltus, the probability that Quinen himself would try to stop Lord Rowen.

She shook her head slowly. "I'm not going with you."

"What do you mean?" asked Michael Rowen.

"I just came to warn you. I felt an obligation to, but I'm not staying around."

"Where do you expect to go?"

"I don't know, but my brother, the Sylvan, and the

wraith all want my death. I can't stay here." She
hesitated, thinking aloud. "Perhaps I'll head west.
There are many new kingdoms in the ruins of
S'Shegan's Empire—there ought to be opportunities.
Perhaps I can sell my sorcery as you do. Or I could
go farther west, to the unexplored lands beyond the
Western League of Kingdoms."

"We need your help against the Sylvan—you know
their ways and their powers, we don't. And Rusty
seems to think you can help us defeat the wraith;
that's one reason why he helped you back at Carlton."

As Rowen paused, Leah glanced over at the precog.
So that was why he had helped her. What had he
foreseen?

"I'm sure that we can convince your brother that
he was wrong about you," Rowen continued.

Leah shook her head. "Even so, there's the wraith
to consider. I don't know how I can help defeat it.
The programmed spellstone it planted at Carlton almost destroyed my half-brother, even with our aid.
The wraithstone I ran into would have killed me if
I'd been a little less lucky. But what scares me more
is that the wraith itself is far more powerful than its
programmed stones. I don't want to meet it."

"If we don't eliminate Shaltus, you'll never be safe
no matter where you go," replied Rowen. "It would
send other stones out to find you. You'd be forced to
fight it someday. Why not do it now, with us? We can
help each other."

Leah shivered, sensing the truth in what Rowen
said. And even if she could be free of the wraith, the
thought of making her way alone in the world terrified
her. For most of her life she'd had her father and her
grandfather to protect her; now they were gone. She
felt lost and alone. There was no longer a place for
her.

Perhaps Rowen could make her half-brother accept

the truth about what had happened so that she could return to Carlton. In many ways her life there had not been a happy one, but sometimes an unpleasant certainty was more preferable than the unknown.

Of course, there might be a certain amount of satisfaction in showing Richard just how wrong he was about her by helping destroy Shaltus.

But why should she risk her life for those who despised her? She had fulfilled her obligation to her father; she had none to her half-brother, none. Let him aid Rowen in destroying the wraith; why should she have to face its power?

Suddenly she had no real reasons to stay, only reasons to go.

Rowen was now talking with Klaus and the other Carlton soldier. He turned to the soldier and said, "I want you to ride to Castle Carlton and tell Lord Richard what's happened. Warn him about the Sylvan and the possibility that another programmed spellstone will be planted in the castle. Explain that Leah warned us."

Rusty frowned. "Then you are determined to go after Lady Barbara?"

"I think we have to," replied Michael Rowen.

As the soldier bid farewell to Klaus, Leah walked over to Michael Rowen.

"But how will you manage against the Sylvan?" she asked.

"You can help us with that."

"But I've decided I'm not going with you."

Suddenly Rowen reached forward and took her hand. His huge hands were gentle but unyielding. "Of course you are." His eyes were warm silver-gray flecked with jade.

Disconcerted by the friendliness, sincerity, and certainty in his eyes, she glanced away. Though the pressure on her hand was as soft as a breeze, her fingers seemed to burn in his grasp. She felt flustered and self-conscious.

"We need you," he said. "We can help one another." He seemed totally sincere.

The thought of someone, especially him, needing her impressed her even more than the thought of facing the Shaltus-wraith or of running from it forever.

Her weak resolve to leave crumbled. It was not totally rational to stay, but somehow she could no longer go.

She nodded, staring mutely at the ground, feeling too uneasy to meet his steady gaze.

"Good," said Rowen. He turned to the others. "Let's get going, we have little time. If we are going to avoid Ravensclife, we'll have to take that side trail. Rusty, you better show me exactly where you think we'll find the Sylvan and Lady Barbara."

Releasing Leah's hand with a squeeze, he strode over to the map.

She stood still, trying to pull her scattered thoughts into some kind of order, while the warmth in her hand seemed to spread throughout her body.

Ten

She pushed back long strands of hair plastered against her face with sweat, shaded her eyes, and glanced up at the sky. A light gray film of cloud blotted out most of the blue. It half-veiled the sun, turning it into a tarnished coin that flared into gold or almost disappeared whenever the obscuring cover shifted.

For hours the air had been heavy with the threat of thunderstorms that never materialized. Several times the clouds to the north had thickened and darkened, only to fade quickly back into light gray. Now thunderheads were building again in the mountains behind them.

Leah wished that it would rain and break the muggy heat that had accompanied them during the two days since they'd left the Bluefield Road.

She looked up the trail and found her eyes drawn to the large figure of Michael Rowen riding in the lead. She studied his thick shoulders and broad back. He looked relaxed, but a slight stiffness in his bearing made her think that he was at full attention, ready for anything.

Timothy Fletcher moved his brown gelding alongside her chestnut mare. He gestured at the long mountain ridge to the north where the sky was darkening. "That would be White Oak Mountain. We've almost reached Bluestone Lake."

"Do you think there'll be a storm?" she asked, glancing again at the massing clouds.

"Maybe in an hour or two, but that one's moving east. I don't think it will reach us."

"I hope it rains soon," said Leah. She shifted uncomfortably. Her body was stiff and sore from riding, her damp clothes stuck to her body, and her skin itched from numerous mosquito bites.

"N'Omb's damnation!" she exclaimed, reaching forward to brush a tick from her leg. Fortunately the bug was just crawling along the surface of her trousers, so it was easy to remove. However, she didn't doubt that later she'd find that several of the insects had gotten beneath her clothing, for they'd been riding through a meadow of shoulder-high weeds and grasses for some time. There ought to be a spell to keep such pests away, she thought, but if there was one she didn't know about it.

The meadow gave way to marshes, and suddenly the bright blue of the lake was ahead of them. They could see the northern shoreline curving to the east where it met the Greenstone River. The lake was long and narrow, only a few times wider than a river.

A long-deserted farmhouse stood about a half a kilometer to the north. Its roof was caved in, and its wooden sides were stripped of paint. They looked ready to tumble in after the roof at any moment. At the intersection of the lake and river stood a cluster of other structures, probably the remains of a tiny village.

An old wagon trail, now overgrown, paralleled the lakeside.

The party crossed the road, dismounted at the edge of the lake, and watered their animals. While the rest of the group bathed faces and refilled canteens, Michael Rowen wandered back to the road. Leah found herself watching him from the corner of her eye as she splashed herself with the cooling water. Her gaze kept drifting to his hands; she remembered how small hers had seemed within them.

"Tim, over here," he called. Fletcher dried his face on the sleeve of his light cotton shirt, slipped his spectacles back on, and walked over to the road.

The two men studied the ground. Apparently they'd found some fresh tracks.

Klaus looked up with interest, finished refilling his canteen, and strode over to them.

"What have you found?" he asked.

"It looks like a party of horsemen passed by here less than an hour ago. The horses were large ones carrying heavy loads," said Fletcher.

The lieutenant scratched his several-days-old beard thoughtfully. "The Sylvan?"

"It looks like it."

Michael Rowen stooped over to study the hoof-prints once more. He picked up a loose stone that looked lost inside his large hands and absentmindedly tossed it back and forth. Straightening abruptly, he hurled the rock toward the lake. It skipped across the water several times before sinking.

Then he called to Leah and Rusty. "We'd better get going. I'll ride on ahead as scout."

In a few minutes the rest of the group followed him.

"How many Sylvan were there?" asked Leah as her horse came abreast of Fletcher's.

"Eight. It looks as though one of them is carrying Lady Barbara."

Leah glanced back at the precog. He'd been drinking heavily ever since his trance, and he'd grown withdrawn and uncommunicative. "We may have to carry Rusty soon, at the rate he's going."

"He'll be all right. Michael, Rusty, and I have been a team for a long time. I've learned that Rusty is never quite as drunk as he appears to be, or as he'd like to be, for that matter."

"How long have you been with Lord Rowen?"

"About six years. He's known Rusty longer than that."

Leah studied Fletcher's face, noting his high cheekbones, long nose, and deepset brown eyes, which were partially obscured by gold wire-rimmed glasses. She wondered how he fit into a team of sorcerer and precog, and she wondered if he really did carry a copy of The Book of Revelations.

"How did you come to join him?" she asked.

Fletcher frowned slightly and looked away. "It's a long story. I guess I'm a misfit like Rusty and Michael, but somehow we all seem to fit together."

"A misfit? I can understand why you'd say that about Rusty. He's a precog who doesn't want to be one. But I don't see why you and Lord Rowen are misfits."

"I told you that I'm a scholar. I guess I've always been more interested in the past than in the present." He looked uncomfortable.

"I'm out of step with the world, that's all."

Sensing that he didn't want to talk about himself, Leah asked, "What about Rowen? He's reputed to be one of the most powerful sorcerers around."

"But he's a sorcerer without a kingdom," answered Fletcher with a sad smile. "He may be the best, but he has to wander like some sort of itinerant pedlar selling his wares. The rest of the great sorcerers have land, wealth, power."

"Wasn't there a kingdom of Rowen once?"

"Yes. It was destroyed in the Great War with S'Shegan. Most of the S'Rowen family were killed. Michael is probably the last of them. He's a Rowen now, not a S'Rowen, for there is no kingdom left. It lay almost in the center of the badlands."

Leah shivered, thinking of the area where most of the battles of the Great War had been fought twenty years ago. There had been castles there once, and farms and forests. But the area had been devastated by fighting, fire, and sorcery. The latter had done the most damage, as spell upon spell altered the land into a barren wasteland of deserts, canyons, and even volcanoes. It was said that wraiths, runespells, and spots of evil magic remained in some areas. The badlands were cursed. There were no farms there now, no castles, no kingdoms.

"Michael could have used his powers to gain a kingdom, someone else's of course. It happens all the time. But that is just not his way." Fletcher sighed. "Sometimes he seems happy enough to be free of the responsibilities, but I know that deep down he'd like to be a lord in more than name. Perhaps that's why he's so eager to rescue your sister."

"How's that?"

"Oh, you must know that Lord S'Carlton has hinted that if Michael destroys the wraith he'll arrange a marriage between him and Lady Barbara. They'd be given Castle Bluefield and all the land reclaimed from the wraith."

"What?" Leah's stomach twisted into a knot that wound tighter and tighter. She was surprised more by her feeling of distress than by the arrangement itself. An alliance between the S'Carltons and a great sorcerer like Rowen made a lot of sense, even if he had no kingdom of his own. Why did it upset her?

She forced herself to speak calmly. "No, I didn't know that. Interesting."

"So you can see why Michael chose to go after Lady Barbara and ignore Rusty's warnings. Under other circumstances he probably would have taken Rusty's advice. We've learned to rely on it."

The trail suddenly angled away from the lake,

curved sharply downhill, and crossed over a wooden bridge spanning a fast-moving stream—the Bluestone River. On the opposite bank the road forked, with one path continuing southward parallel to the lake, the other meandering alongside the river.

Michael Rowen had halted by the fork and was examining the ground. "It looks like the Sylvan have split into two groups," he said when they reached him.

Tim prodded his horse forward, circled, and inspected both routes.

"I can't tell which one is the group with Lady Barbara. Both trails eventually go to Bluefield."

"Can't you see any difference in the tracks?" asked Klaus.

"They've evidently paired the Lady with one of the smaller Sylvan so that all the horses are carrying about the same weight."

"Leah, can you sense anything?" said Rowen, looking at her thoughtfully.

She avoided his gaze, wondering why it made her feel uncomfortable. Cupping her spellstone in her hands, she sought contact with her half-sister or the Sylvan, but they were out of her range.

She shook her head.

"Then we'd better split up," decided Rowen. "Tim, you and Leah follow the stream. Rusty, Klaus, and I will keep to the lake road. If you determine that they don't have Barbara, double back and join us. We'll do the same. If they have her, keep following them, but don't start anything until we rejoin you. For all we know these Sylvan could have another of Shaltus's damned programmed stones. If so, I doubt a single sorcerer could defeat them."

"Their horses aren't moving very fast," added Fletcher. "The tracks indicate that the animals have been traveling hard and are getting pretty tired. It shouldn't take too long to catch up to them."

"You'd better take some more of the *tomaad* from my pack horse," said Leah. Each of the party already had taken a full canteen, but now that they were separating it seemed prudent to divide the supply of the drug more equitably.

"That's a good idea." Rowen smiled at her as he helped himself to a cask of *tomaad*. He looped another canteen of the drug over Rusty's shoulder. The precog looked drunk and not much interested in what was going on.

"Give me another canteen too," said Fletcher.

Leah removed a flask from her pack horse and passed it to him. He pulled the strap over his head so that the canteen hung across his chest.

Leah glanced back at Rowen. The sorcerer was still looking at her with a warm smile. She smiled back shyly and looked quickly away.

"Good luck," said Rowen.

"Good hunting," Tim Fletcher called back.

Then the two groups separated.

"It seems odd that the Sylvan party split up," remarked Fletcher, leading the way down the rather wide trail that ran along the bank of the Bluestone.

Leah prodded her horse into a trot alongside his gelding. "I know. There's nothing out this way except for Bluefield. Where would they be going except there? They wouldn't have sent out a hunting party either. The Sylvan carry their own supply of food since their diet consists primarily of skytree nuts and sap, and they eat very little meat."

"Could it be that they realize we are following them, and they've split up so that we would also separate?"

"It's a possibility," Leah replied.

Frowning, Fletcher nodded at the confirmation of his suspicion.

He pulled up the sword that hung from the front

of his saddle, unsheathed the blade, and laid it across his knees.

"It's too bad Rusty didn't *see* anything today," he said.

Leah smiled. "In his condition he was lucky to see the road." She turned toward Fletcher. "Why does he drink so much, anyway? Why doesn't he want to use his abilities?"

Fletcher pushed his glasses back against the bridge of his nose and glanced at her thoughtfully. "I guess it's no secret. He was an advisor to the S'Rowens, the S'Yorks, and some of the other nobles during the Great War. He used his precognition to plan battle strategies against S'Shegan—and they were successful."

"He didn't drink then?"

"No. I've heard that his powers were really remarkable in those days. He could have looked at a road like this and told us what we'd meet at every bend and curve in it for the next twenty kilometers. He was evidently instrumental in devising the plan that finally destroyed S'Shegan. However, he didn't notice that among all its rippling side effects was one that would involve a small town in what was left of the kingdom of Rowen. Castle Rowen itself had already been destroyed. There was a skirmish near the village. S'Shegan's men captured the area and destroyed the town. Rusty's wife and children were there."

"They were killed?" she asked.

"Yes. But you see, they wouldn't have been if Rusty hadn't used his powers and acted on what he saw. He blames himself for what happened."

Leah nodded. "He must be afraid to use his powers. That's what he was talking about when he tried to explain his precognition to us. He didn't want to give us advice because he might have overlooked one of the variables and ended up sending us into a danger greater than the one he was warning us about."

"That's it. But in all the years I've known him he's never steered me wrong."

"I wish you hadn't said that," Leah replied with a wry smile, "considering that all he was able to foretell was that we were riding into danger and probably wouldn't be able to save Barbara anyway."

Lightning flashed in the sky behind them. Thunder pealed. Leah's mare shied at the sound. She leaned forward, stroked its coarse brown mane, and soothed it with a soft mental command.

"It looks like we might get some of that rain yet," said Fletcher. He slowed his horse to examine the tracks once more. "We seem to be catching up to them. Can you sense anything?"

Murmuring a spell, Leah searched the area for signs of the Sylvan. She felt a faint stirring. "Barbara . . ." she said aloud. Then the feeling faded. She closed her eyes, striving to renew contact, but she was only aware of where Barbara had been. It was like following a whiff of perfume. "There . . ." She opened her eyes and found herself pointing to the northwest, away from the path of the river they followed.

"What? Are you sure of that?" asked Fletcher.

"I've always been especially sensitive to my siblings. I don't think I could be mistaken. Maybe they've turned off this trail."

"But why would they head away from Bluefield?" Fletcher leaned down to study the tracks again. Then he prodded his gelding into a swift trot.

When they'd gone several kilometers farther, Fletcher pulled up abruptly, dismounted, and again examined the ground.

"They have turned off—here." He gestured toward the rocky slope of an old creek bed that headed northward, back into the mountains. The stream was almost dry, with only a narrow gully filled with fast-moving water. "All four horsemen."

"Why have they gone this way?" asked Leah.

"I don't know. If they realized that we were following them, they may have wanted to throw us off their trail. It looks pretty rocky. It will be hard to follow their tracks." He remounted. "We'd better keep after them before the rain washes out what prints there are."

Leah studied the black clouds. The new path headed right into the storm. Bolts of lightning cracked the sky a few kilometers ahead.

It was still oppressively hot, but Leah shivered. She felt suddenly tense and apprehensive.

They followed the creek along a ravine that gradually deepened into a steep-walled canyon. As it began to rain, the creek quickly overflowed the gully and began to widen toward its old banks.

Leah concentrated on following the faint impression that Barbara and the Sylvan rode somewhere ahead of them. She called out to Fletcher.

"Even if the rain destroys the tracks, I think we'll be able to follow them. Barbara's just on the edge of my range, and we should be closing in on the group."

"Good. But I wonder how Michael's going to track us if this . . ."

His words became a cry of surprise.

A dark shape had launched itself at him from somewhere in the rocks above.

At that moment something slammed into Leah's back. Her horse screamed and reared in fright. Leah twisted against ripping claws, lost her balance, and fell to the ground.

Instantly the beast was on top of her.

Impressions of tawny fur, her fingers digging into a dirty white throat to keep the small head and discolored teeth from her neck, black patches of fur on each side of the muzzle, golden eyes with narrow black slits, claws raking her arms.

A puma.

Her spellstone flared into life. Her protective shield pushed back the cat. She reached for its mind and felt the will of another. A Sylvan had it under control.

She cried a spell that hurled a bolt of energy into its chest. As it collapsed, the smell of its singed fur blended with the musky cat odor.

She caught sight of Fletcher, sword in hand, standing over the body of another cat. A third circled him warily and then sprang for the kill. His blade flashed and cut into the golden body.

Something moved at the edge of her vision. She turned toward it and met its frenzied roar with a murmured incantation. Her spell caught the male puma and silenced it as it fell.

Now there was only the noise of the storm that had hit as they fought.

Leah stood and surveyed the canyon. Four cats lay dead. There were no signs of others. She probed the area for the Sylvan, but they were out of her range now, and the trace of Barbara's presence had vanished as well.

Fletcher stood a few meters away with his back to the wind, his head tilted upward, and his sword extended. He let the rain wash the blood from the scratches on his face and arms and from the edge of his blade.

Lightning struck somewhere nearby, fully illuminating the storm-darkened canyon. The horses were gone—stampeded by fear back the way they had come.

As Leah tried to contact them telepathically, another bolt hit, lighting the area. Leah noticed the stream. It had become a raging torrent of water fed by the rain funneling down through the mountains. It had overflowed the old bank of the stream and was rising rapidly toward the edge of the canyon floor where they stood. Remembering the steep walls of the ravine, Leah felt a surge of panic.

"Fletcher, are you all right?" she said, running over to him.

"Yes."

"Look at the water." She pointed. It was already beginning to lap at their heels.

"Where are the horses?"

Leah frowned, concentrated once more on locating the animals, and found nothing. "Stampeded. They are out of my range to control them."

Fletcher grabbed her arm and pulled her toward the side of the canyon. "We'll have to climb. This flood could trap us."

Leah scrambled up the rain-slick boulders at the canyon wall. She turned to help the shorter man as the climb became steeper.

"I hope we don't run into more of those mountain lions," Fletcher said. "Strange that so many should attack like that, and in this storm too."

Leah shook her head. "They were under Sylvan control. Some Sylvan have the ability to communicate with and control animals. They act as the tribe's defenders, protecting the forest from wild animals and using their telepathic ability to hunt for game. Evidently one of the Sylvan we're trailing is a defender."

"Could he attack again?"

"It's unlikely that there are more cats nearby that he could use. Besides, the defenders usually can't 'path over more than a few kilometers. I don't sense anyone that close to us now."

Fletcher brushed his sodden hair back from his face, flicked raindrops from his spectacles with his fingertips, and stared at the muddy flood of water below them.

"But I thought some Sylvan could telepath for hundreds of kilometers?"

"A few specially trained ones can, with each other. They are the communicators who maintain contact between the Sylvan forests. However, they can't control animals at that range."

"Hey, there's a cave!" Fletcher cried, as he searched for their best path upward. "I don't think the water will reach that high. We can use some shelter from this storm."

Leah followed as he ascended, but she didn't see the opening until several bright bursts of lightning illuminated the dark recess. There seemed to be some sort of writing on the rocks edging it, but she couldn't be sure.

At last they reached the crevice. They were high above the river and out of reach of its flood waters.

Leah grabbed Fletcher's arm as lightning flashed again. Now she could clearly see the writing that outlined the cave opening.

"We can't go in there!" She pointed to the script and designs. "It's a forbidden place of N'Omb."

"Apparently," replied Fletcher without concern. He studied with equal interest the warnings that she could read and the ancient writing she could not. Then he turned to enter the cave.

"It's a taboo place." She shouted against the force of the storm and the indoctrinated fear she felt at the thought of entering a place forbidden to all except the highest of the N'Omb priests.

Fletcher turned to her and smiled gently. "It's all right. There's nothing to fear inside."

"How do you know?" she asked, astonished that he could think calmly of entering a place that the N'Omb Church had declared off limits. Even the nonbelieving Sylvan left N'Omb forbidden areas strictly alone.

"Do you sense anything dangerous?" he said, avoiding her question with one of his own.

She pressed her fingers against the powerstone and probed the cave psychically. There seemed to be no magic, no animals, no danger—only a cave.

Still warily eyeing the man-sized crevice, she shook her head.

Fletcher took her hand. "Come on. We need shelter from this storm—or would you prefer to stay out on this ledge?"

Leah shifted uncomfortably inside her drenched garments. The storm showed no signs of abating. The rain was cold and hard, and the lightning continued to hit distressingly near.

She nervously clutched her spellstone as Tim led her into the cave. She tried not to be afraid, but she'd been taught enough of the N'Omb religion to fear the unknown consequences of breaking its taboos.

The narrow crevice angled downward for a few meters and then widened into what seemed to be a large cave.

As Leah sagged wearily into a corner, Fletcher produced some matches from his belt-pouch and lit one. The flame's weak light didn't push away much of the gloom, but it was enough to reveal unnaturally smooth, moss-covered walls and scattered debris of leaves and rocks on the level floor.

"I'm sorry," said Leah, striving to bring herself back into control. She stood, lifted her spellstone over her head, murmured a spell, and said "I wasn't thinking," as the gem started to glow with the light of many candles.

Except for the smoothness of the walls, the place seemed like a natural cave.

Despite the grim N'Omb warnings against trespass Leah's fear began to ease. She began to take stock of their situation. She realized that they would have to do something about their wet clothes or risk catching cold in the coolness of the cave. There was no spell to dry the clothes directly, but perhaps she could improvise.

She focused on her stone and chanted. Suddenly a warm breeze began to blow in the center of the room, bringing up a whirl of leaves as it flowed. The debris spun faster; the breeze became a hot, dry wind.

"What?" Fletcher gasped.

"To dry our clothes," Leah replied. She glanced at him. For the first time she noticed the flask still hanging across his chest.

"We should drink some of that *tomaad*," she said. "It will heal these cat scratches and keep them from becoming infected."

"Of course." Fletcher looked at the canteen with mild surprise, as though he'd forgotten he carried it. He took a long swallow and passed it to Leah.

The *tomaad* was cool and refreshing. It had the sweetness of honey without its thick, cloying texture, and had a nutlike flavor.

The pain from the bites and scratches faded. A feeling of energy and well-being replaced Leah's fatigue.

For a few minutes they stood silently in the center of the cave, letting the *tomaad* take full effect while the hot wind blew them dry. When it had, Leah ended the spell.

She probed the area again for any signs of Barbara and the Sylvan. She found nothing. They were probably heading for Bluefield. It seemed unlikely that she, Fletcher, or the others would be able to catch them now.

She glanced at the too-smooth walls and floor of the chamber once more. Her curiosity about the place overrode her fear of the N'Omb warnings. Cautiously circling the room, she noted that the crevice was apparently a natural opening caused by a long-ago rockfall, but the room itself was man-made. An archway at the far end of the room opened onto a passageway leading deeper into the cliff.

"What is this place anyway?" she asked Fletcher. He'd been certain that it was safe to enter. Evidently he knew something about it.

"A worship place for the N'Omb priests now," he replied, his voice a bit too casual.

"And what was it before? You said you were interested in the past. Is that how you knew this place was not dangerous?"

He looked uncomfortably away. "It's ancient, carved before the time of N'Omb. I think men hid here when the fires of N'Omb fell. That's why the Church has made it a taboo-place. They fear the knowledge of the past. But it's safe here. Any secrets this place contained were found and destroyed long ago."

"Destroyed?"

Fletcher's voice turned hard. His face grew grave, as though he disapproved. "For thousands of years the Church destroyed all relics of the past. This place was probably found and cleaned out then. But in more recent times the philosophy of the Church has changed somewhat, and some artifacts from N'Omb's time are preserved as holy relics. Now a few places such as this are kept as the holiest of holy shrines. Of course, anything that the Church thinks is potentially dangerous is still destroyed."

He sighed. "What a waste. The learning of the ancients has been systematically erased from the face of the earth. The few things that remain are shrouded in silly superstition and myth."

"How do you know all this?" Leah asked. "Is it because you are a scholar?" She remembered The Book of Revelations she's seen, and she made a quick guess. "Or because you are a priest?"

Fletcher scowled. "What makes you think that?"

"I saw the copy of The Book of Revelations that you carry."

"Oh." Fletcher shrugged. "You might as well know. I was a priest once. I was a Church historian." Now that she'd guessed his secret he seemed suddenly eager to talk about it.

"The beginnings of Church history fascinated me. I was such a fine scholar that I was even sent to the White Tower of N'Omb to study. I spent several years there researching the most ancient documents in its vast library. I found some things that contradicted the very heart of Church doctrine. When I began to question my superiors and the recognized dogma, I was demoted and divested of my spellstone. I continued to question things and eventually was dismissed."

His voice echoed the frustration and anger he must have felt. Then his tone changed and became almost boastful. "So I had to continue my studies outside the Church. I've learned some incredible things about the ancients. They once had vast cities of cement, steel, and glass. And a science that made sorcery look like child's play. If only I could find more clues to its working, I could recreate it. However, the Church has destroyed everything." He smiled a shy, secretive smile. "Well, almost everything."

Leah felt a wave of shock as she realized what he was urging. She did not even know the meaning of the word *science*, but whatever it was, it was the most dangerous of all things in the world, and the most forbidden. The mention of the word itself in public was still a death sentence in some human lands. She only knew of it from something that Trask had said once, but even the Sylvan forbade any attempts to study it. According to the legends, N'Omb had almost destroyed the world to punish men for its use. . . .

"You mustn't speak of such things," she cried out.

In a way she was suddenly more afraid of Fletcher than she had ever been of Shaltus.

"I'm sorry," he said. "You're right, I got carried away. Much of the old knowledge is dangerous. Perhaps there is wisdom in letting the world forget it. But I'm a seeker of knowledge, and I must keep searching for it for my own sake, even if others would forbid it." Realizing her fear, he sighed and said, "I won't speak of it again."

Leah nodded. She edged away from him to look out the cave opening. "The rain is still coming down hard, and the valley has become a river. We'd better get some rest while we can."

"Right." By unspoken agreement Fletcher moved toward the back of the chamber while Leah sat down near the entrance.

"I'll set up wards against intrusion," said Leah.

She recited an incantation and used her stone to trace a pattern of runes in the dirt floor. When she finished its light dimmed into a warming glow.

She curled up on the floor and tried to sleep, but she couldn't relax. Fletcher's strange ideas were bewildering and disturbing.

She wondered if Michael Rowen knew of them and then decided he must. If Fletcher did know something of the forbidden science, as he'd hinted, had he used it in the past to supplement the sorcerer's power? Was that how he fit into the team of sorcerer and precog?

She shuddered at the thought. The tales of N'Omb's fiery destruction of most of the earth, even if only half-true, were enough to convince anyone of the necessity of forbidding the old ways.

Quinen was willing to use any means to gain his ends. Was Rowen?

Quinen. Strange, she hadn't really thought about him since she'd joined Lord Rowen's group. It seemed as if what had happened between them had been only a dream that would fade away with time.

She wondered what Quinen had thought when he'd discovered her escape. Was it possible that a part of him had been glad? She wanted to think so.

Where was Quinen now? She hoped that they would not meet again. Yet it was conceivable that he would ride to Bluefield to try to stop Rowen. She might have to fight him.

Quinen's face came suddenly and unbidden into her mind's eye. He was as she had seen him in sleep. His face was unlined, untroubled. His features were boyish and innocent, a handsome mask that gave no clue to the inner man.

She remembered him kissing her; even then there had been a hardness in his mismatched eyes of silver and brown.

Suddenly the face she imagined altered, and the eyes became warm and gray. Strong, gentle hands touched hers and then pulled her close.

She blinked and pulled away from the daydream of herself in Michael Rowen's arms.

What was the matter with her? First she'd gotten involved with Quinen, and now she felt attracted to Rowen. Where was the control she'd always had over her emotions?

How could she be attracted to such dissimilar men anyway? One was human and one was Sylvan, and their personalities were entirely different.

Perhaps they were alike in some ways, however. Both were large, powerful men. Both were men of power. And power hungry, she reminded herself. Even Rowen—she thought of the deal he'd made with her half-brother to win a kingdom for himself. He would marry Barbara—if she lived.

Leah tried to shut off the flow of thoughts. She needed to sleep while she had the opportunity. She forced herself to concentrate on her spellstone. Its glow seemed to beat against her eyelids with a hypnotic rhythm as her mind linked with it.

But as she fell asleep, her last thought was of the feeling of Rowen's large hands pressed against hers.

Eleven

It wasn't until morning that the flood waters below the cave receded enough for Leah and Fletcher to leave. They had no choice except to backtrack to the Bluestone River, where they might find their horses and meet up with Rowen's group. Having failed to intercept the Sylvan, they'd have to return to their original plan to reach Bluefield and destroy the Shaltus-wraith, if they could.

They found Leah's packhorse about three kilometers downstream. Its bloated carcass lay among the mudsoaked debris scattered along the path of the flood. The packs were gone, evidently washed away when the animal had been caught in the flood.

By the time they reached the Bluestone, Leah had about given up hope of finding their mounts alive. But as they stood surveying the river, Michael Rowen's party arrived, leading both the gelding and the mare.

"Thanks be to N'Omb," Rowen exclaimed. The sorcerer grinned at Leah, dismounted, and clasped Fletcher's arm warmly. "We were worried when we found these horses of yours grazing back at the fork. What happened?"

While Fletcher told the others of their adventures, Leah studied the group. Klaus's leg was bandaged, Rusty looked haggard and almost sober, and Rowen had several new, half-healed scratches and cuts on his arms.

Michael Rowen nodded. "Something similar happened to us. First the Sylvan cut off the road and headed into a maze of narrow canyons. Suddenly we were attacked by a pack of wolves. It started to rain, and we lost the Sylvan's trail. We wandered around until dark trying to pick it up, then decided to head back to you this morning."

"The Sylvan must have reached Bluefield by now," said Fletcher.

Klaus frowned. "Then Lady Barbara is lost."

"It would seem so," replied Rowen.

"There's no reason for you to come any farther, Lieutenant Klaus. We're almost at Bluefield now. As a nonsorcerer you'd be more of a liability than a help within the wraith's province. You'd better ride back to Carlton and inform Lord S'Carlton."

The lieutenant looked relieved. He didn't want to get any closer to Bluefield than necessary. "All right. If you are sure you don't need me?"

"Lord Richard only sent you along as a guide. Leah knows the wraith's territory as well as anyone, so she can lead us."

Klaus eyed Leah suspiciously. "If that's what you want."

"I think it would be best."

"May N'Omb bless you and protect you," said the lieutenant. "I don't mind telling you I'm just as happy to be out of this."

As he rode out, the rest of the group headed south along the Bluestone trail.

Soon the forest thickened around them, choking the river into a trickle of water, hiding the bright blue sky with a dark canopy of leaves, and plunging the pathway into shadowed gloom.

The hairs on the back of Leah's neck prickled. The air had become suffocatingly hot and heavy. There was a feeling of foreboding about the forest, as though it were trying to tell them to turn back.

Their horses slowed, involuntarily responding to the insidious warning.

Leah and Rowen were both at full alert. They used their spellstones to probe the area ahead.

The trees around them began to change. They were no longer straight-limbed plants arched toward the sky. Now the trunks were twisted, the limbs gnarled, the bark mottled with unhealthy looking patches of fungus. Streamers of moss hung from some of the branches, hiding the sun even more.

The trunks leaned away from the vertical. They were slanted toward Bluefield, as though pulled by an unseen force.

Leah listened in vain for the call of a bird or the chitter of a squirrel. An unnatural silence pervaded the area.

Suddenly Michael Rowen signaled the group to halt.

"There's something up ahead . . ." he warned.

Leah studied the woods, but she sensed only a quiet emptiness. Fletcher and Rusty unsheathed their swords.

They waited expectantly.

Prodding his horse into position next to Leah's, Rowen thrust his huge right hand toward her. "Link," he commanded.

She touched his hand timidly and then gripped it as the energy flow between them built into a protective pattern around the four of them.

The physical touch enabled them to link on an empathic level, not a telepathic one, but it was enough to allow Leah to focus on what Rowen had sensed.

Somewhere along the trail ahead a shielded area was moving toward them. The barrier had been cleverly erected so that it reflected the world around it, concealing whatever or whoever was inside and making psychic detection of its presence difficult. As it moved there was only a slight rippling effect that distinguished it from the rest of the forest.

Rowen cautiously probed the shield. Gradually both he and Leah began to sense what lay beneath.

There were eight Sylvan on horseback returning from having delivered Barbara to the Shaltus-wraith. One of them carried another programmed wraith-stone; it was producing the protective distort around them.

"No," cried Leah, as she sensed Rowen tensing to attack.

He looked at her sharply.

"We mustn't attack. It would take us too long to break the shield. In the meantime the Sylvan could be using their powers against us." She gestured at the thick trees surrounding them. "They could turn every branch or twig in the area into arms capable of tearing us from limb to limb in seconds."

His keen gray eyes surveyed her critically. Then he nodded.

He called softly to the others, "Get into the woods. We don't want to be seen."

As they reached cover, Rowen altered the shield around them into a distort of the type the wraithstone used. Leah clamped a tight mental hold on the horses so that they would make no sound.

"What's going on?" whispered Tim Fletcher.

"Sssshhh, Sylvan are coming this way," Rowen explained.

They held their breaths and watched the trail.

Suddenly Rusty stood up. His forehead beaded with sweat, his eyes began to roll up in their sockets, and his hands shook.

Simultaneously Leah and Rowen grabbed the precog and forced him to the ground. He moaned in his trance. Rowen covered Rusty's mouth with his hand to stifle the sound.

Muffled hoofbeats broke the forest's deathlike silence.

As Leah and Rowen cradled Rusty's squirming body, their fingers intertwined in readiness. Wordlessly they each understood that if the wraithstone sensed their presence they'd only have time for one united strike against it.

Then the Sylvan appeared. A protective field surrounded them with a cloud of golden light.

They galloped by and disappeared from view.

The precog shuddered and twisted violently.

Rowen smiled reassuringly at Leah as Rusty's eyes blinked and glared at them. When the hoofbeats had faded, Rowen removed his hand.

"What were you doing that for?" said Rusty indignantly. "Can't a man daydream in peace?"

"Not if he's going to groan about it," Michael Rowen replied. Standing, he helped the older man to his feet. "*See* anything of interest?"

"Not much." Rusty shrugged.

"Come on, that's the longest you've been out in quite a while. You must have seen something."

"The Shaltus-wraith wields a lot of power. Now that we're in its territory it fogs what I can see. I can tell you one thing though. Our expedition is a node in the timelines. Its outcome casts an almost infinite series of ripple-effects on the future."

"You can do better than that."

Rusty brushed off his trousers, removed a flask from his pocket, and took a long sip of the liquor.

"The probabilities look good," he said. "But the wraith will have a lot of tricks up his sleeve. He's a master of illusion and nonillusion. You'll have to determine which is which. He'll use your weaknesses against you, and you must use his weakness against him."

"His weakness?" asked Leah. She didn't know the wraith had one.

"His hatred of the S'Carltons is both a strength and a weakness. Cut him with it before he cuts you."

"Can you speak in nothing but generalities?" exclaimed Fletcher.

"It's better that I do. To know the future and to act on it is to change it, and what if it were changed for the worst?"

"Then you think we will destroy the wraith?" Michael Rowen asked.

The precog smiled enigmatically. "It's best if I say no more, except for one word of warning—don't get separated."

"What of Fletcher's plan?"

Rusty's lips drew into a firm line. His words sounded definite. "I see no alternative to it."

"What plan?" asked Leah.

Casually sitting cross-legged on the trail, Michael Rowen gestured to the others. They followed his example and sat across from him.

"The wraith seems to be more powerful than Shaltus ever was in life and perhaps more powerful than any human sorcerer is or can be. Therefore either the wraith is capable of drawing on more energy than we are, or it has found some manner of storing it in great quantities, which it can tap at will."

"Runes can be used to store energy," said Leah.

"Yes, but the energy leaks away after a few hours if the runespell isn't activated." Rowen looked thoughtful. "It would seem that Shaltus is able to tap into far more energy than a mere rune could bind."

"Perhaps a spellstone can transfer and transform energy more efficiently without the linkage between the stone and a controlling human," said Tim Fletcher.

Rowen shrugged. "In any case the Shaltus wraith-stone appears to be far stronger than any sorcerer. So far only sorcery has been used against it, and it has always won the battle of magic against magic." He turned toward Leah. "We propose to destroy the wraith with something else."

Leah jumped to her feet. "The forbidden ways!" Her voice was tight with anger and fear.

Rowen followed as she stalked a few paces away. Taking her hand gently, he studied her face with concern.

"What do you know of this?"

"I'm afraid it's my fault," Fletcher interjected. "When we were stranded in the N'Omb cave yesterday I told Leah that I sought the old knowledge."

Rowen's voice was as calm and reassuring as his deep gray eyes. "There's no need to be afraid. Fletcher has discovered something that we hope to use against Shaltus. It's a small amount of simple powder in a pipelike device that will explode the stone and yet not hurt a person standing a few meters away. It is a secret thing that we will not tell to others, lest it be used for evil. It is the only thing I know of that will destroy the wraithstone."

Rusty stood and patted Leah's shoulder. "The Shaltus-stone must be eliminated, or its power will grow until it consumes all of Carlton. We must use every weapon we have against it."

Leah knew that he was right, but the thought of breaking N'Omb's greatest law still terrified her.

"Don't worry," said Fletcher. "We only have a little of this powder, and it will be used only once—to destroy the wraithstone."

"But how can we even get near the stone?" Leah asked. "Not even my father could get closer than a kilometer to it. He's not the only sorcerer to die trying to get close to it. And this device of yours would have to be placed near the wraithstone, right?"

"Yes. It would have to touch it," Rowen replied.

"Then how. . . ?"

"The Rowens have an immunity to magic," answered Fletcher.

"Not a total immunity," Rowen explained. "As long as I use a spellstone I'm vulnerable, although I do have a certain amount of natural resistance. Without the stone I'm immune to the direct effects of sorcery."

"I don't understand."

"Do you remember when we fought the planted spellstone at Carlton? The wraithstone erected a barrier to cut us off from aiding your brother. I was able to pass through it."

"And I wasn't able to penetrate it," said Leah, remembering the invisible wall that had kept her from reaching Richard.

"My resistance to sorcery enabled me to force my way through. If I hadn't been wearing my stone, I wouldn't have been affected by Shaltus's sorcery at all."

"But you were knocked out when you destroyed the wraithstone."

"As long as I'm in contact with my powerstone, I can be affected by the sorcery that leaks through my link with the stone. Without the stone I'm not affected by spells, runes, forcefields, or illusions."

Leah frowned, still trying to understand. "But you couldn't cast spells either."

"That's right."

"What do you intend to do then? Just remove your spellstone, ride up to the Shaltus-stone, and use Fletcher's accursed powder to destroy the wraith?" Sarcasm edged Leah's voice. She was certain it would not be that simple to eliminate the wraith.

"Something like that," he replied.

"It sounds too easy."

Fletcher tugged thoughtfully at his beard. "What Michael's neglecting to say is that he is not immune to the indirect effects of sorcery. If Shaltus were to set this forest on fire, for example, Michael would not be immune to the heat and flames. So he'll need some assistance in getting close to the wraithstone."

"Me?" asked Leah.

"Both of us," Fletcher replied. "The three of us will get as close to the stone as we can. Michael will be able to protect me against any spells. Then he'll give me his powerstone, and together you and I will protect him."

Leah's eyes widened in surprise. It was highly unusual for one person to use another's stone. After a long period of use the spellstones became attuned to their owners. A stone could be desensitized and transferred to another individual, but it was a long ritual.

Fletcher read her expression. "I was a sorcerer once, with my own stone, so I have the necessary talent. Michael and I have worked out a shortcut to the usual procedures for transferring a stone. We've done it several times before, and it works. I won't be quite as powerful a sorcerer as Michael is, but I should be good enough for our purposes."

"You two may have to distract the wraith while I get within striking distance," added Rowen.

Leah studied the two men. They both seemed quite serious. She vaguely remembered hearing about a family of sorcerers who had been immune to magic and who had been wiped out in the Great War. Evidently it was the S'Rowen family. Michael Rowen was the only survivor.

Although Michael Rowen's scheme seemed wildly improbable, perhaps it was just crazy enough to work.

Certainly her father's direct attack on the wraith had been ineffective.

"Naturally Rusty will have to stay out of the wraith's territory. We won't be able to spare enough power to protect him from Shaltus, and he is no sorcerer." Rowen smiled at her. "So that's what we'll do, unless you have a better plan."

"No, but this one seems crazy," said Leah.

"We're not being foolhardy. We've got a lot going for us—my immunity, Tim's device, your knowledge of the wraith and your abilities, and Rusty's prediction, such as it was. Are you with us?"

Feeling very much as though she had no choice, Leah nodded reluctantly.

"Good. Let's get moving then."

Twelve

A nightmare stretched before them in the once fertile Bluefield Valley. On the hillside below, the forest became a graveyard of barren, leafless skeletons with gaunt, misshapen arms like broken matchsticks.

The air was heavy, oppressive, and stank of rotting vegetation and dead fish. Perhaps the second smell arose from what had once been a wide blue ribbon of river. It was now a dark bog.

The horses whined in terror and tried to bolt. It took all of Leah's skill to still their fear.

"I go no farther," said Rusty. Leah couldn't tell if his decision was based on his precognitive vision or on the dismal scene.

"The blight's gotten larger since I was here last," Leah noted. She pointed west. "We're still some kilometers from Castle Bluefield. I think we should avoid it. The wraithstone lies on this side of the river, some seven or eight kilometers west of the castle."

"You take the lead," said Rowen. He turned to Rusty. "Are you sure you'll be all right by yourself?"

"Quite sure," replied the precog.

Leah fingered her spellstone nervously. Then she erected a weak protective field around herself and her horse. It would be a slight drain on her energy levels, but she wanted to be prepared for any sudden attacks. Glancing back at Rowen and Fletcher, she saw that the sorcerer had followed her example. Now a pale green-gold aura encircled the two men.

As they reached the wasted trees, she sensed Shaltus's presence for the first time. It was as faint as a spider's shadow, and as repellent.

The air seemed to shimmer with shadows. It became molasses-thick, pressing against them with a tangibility that made it difficult to breathe and to move. Looking through it was like looking through water, and the images of sky, stark tree trunks, and each other wavered and grew indistinct.

Unconsciously Leah's hands tightened around the reins and clenched into fists. Her anxiety built as they traveled deeper into dead forest. Her chest tightened, her back stiffened, and her palms began to sweat.

The stench of decay made her want to gag. Its acrid taste filled her mouth. The viscous air felt like slime against her skin.

Her fear grew. Then she remembered feeling the same terror when her father had fought Shaltus. A portion was her own fear, but most came from somewhere outside herself. Her shield could screen out only part of it.

Knowing that this was something of Shaltus's doing lessened the terror that wrapped itself around her like the suffocating coils of a snake.

She diverted more energy into her shield. The pressure of the fear weakened from an almost paralyzing terror into a formless apprehension.

One look at Fletcher's and Rowen's expressions of pinched anxiety told her that they were also fighting Shaltus's insidious attack.

As they moved forward, the pressure of the assault increased. Leah's nerves screamed with tension. She had to master the urge to turn around and gallop back. She wanted to shriek or cry, or even to laugh hysterically against the dread that crashed against her mind in an avalanche of terror.

It became an effort to think clearly, to think of anything besides the raging sense of despair and alarm. She wondered if this was the cause of the madness that affected those who ventured into Bluefield. Without spellstones there was no way to block it.

"Leah, we've got to keep moving," said Rowen through clenched teeth. He was suddenly beside her. She realized that she'd reined her horse.

Fletcher's hands were pressed against his forehead. "Isn't there something we can do to stop this?" His dark skin glistened with perspiration, his eyes had a wild look of panic, and his whole body trembled.

Rowen remained tight-lipped but calm. Evidently his immunity made him partially resistant to the torment.

"I don't know," he replied. "Is it always like this here?"

Leah nodded. She wanted to cry out and had to fight to form her thoughts into coherent words and then to keep them from twisting into a scream as she spoke. "It's the wraith's first line of defense." She took a deep breath. "It's usually enough to stop most people. When we get beyond these trees it will end. Then he'll hit us with something else."

"I can't take much more of this," cried Fletcher.

"What did Rusty say?" mused Rowen. "He'll use your weaknesses against you, and you must use his weaknesses against him?"

"The wraith must be afraid too. He's afraid of us, and he's afraid of the S'Carltons. After all, your father did kill Shaltus. The wraith remembers the torture he underwent and his slow death all too well—that's why it's so intent on vengeance. It fears final extinction. We must try to channel this formless fear back at the wraith, but give it a basis in reality. Let the spellstone of Shaltus know that we are coming to destroy it."

"Is it wise to attack so early? We're still close to eight kilometers away—the stone is almost out of our range," said Leah.

"I don't expect that we can have much effect on the wraithstone at this distance, but it will give us a chance to test its defenses and weaknesses."

He stretched his arms toward Leah and Fletcher. Prodding her horse closer, Leah clasped hands with each of the men. Fletcher grabbed Michael Rowen's hand to complete the circle.

As their protective auras merged into a single field, Leah began a low chant that Fletcher picked up. Although he had no spellstone of his own, he'd been trained as a sorcerer and was now linked with them, adding his strength to theirs. Rowen repeated the chant and channeled the power behind their words into the spell that he hurled against the wraith.

They let the fear assaulting their senses feed into the death fear of their spell, transforming it from a weapon directed at them into a weapon aimed at the Shaltus-wraith.

They seemed to be in a vortex of terrified emotion. Only Rowen's steady control kept them from being blown away in the whirlwind.

Then the pressure of fear against their minds weakened and died away. They continued their offensive for a few more minutes, until they were certain that Shaltus was not going to renew the attack.

At last Rowen nodded and released their hands. "I don't think we were hurting the wraith, but it didn't like being on the receiving end of a fear-spell."

"Shaltus will try something else now," said Leah. "It may be anything. The wraith always varies its subsequent attacks if the first does not succeed." Feeling shaken and weak, she pulled out her canteen. "I think we should fortify ourselves with *tomaad*. It is one advantage we have that my father didn't."

Rowen nodded. "It's a good thing you thought to divide the *tomaad* among us. Otherwise most would have been lost with your packhorse." He smiled at her. "I'm glad you're with us. You've been a help in many ways."

Blushing, Leah shrugged and looked away. She felt both embarrassed and pleased by his praise. It had been a long time since anyone had complimented her.

Fletcher wiped the perspiration from his brow. Now that Shaltus's assault had ceased he seemed to have regained his composure. "I think we make a good team," he said.

"Yes, we do," Rowen agreed. "Things have gone well so far, except for losing Barbara. I just wish we had been able to save her."

Leah sighed unhappily. The wraith must have killed Barbara as soon as she'd entered its territory. That meant Michael Rowen had lost his chance for a kingdom. Perhaps he had loved Barbara. She wondered which loss disturbed him more.

"I'm sorry," she said, and she was—sorry for him and sorry for her poor half-sister. Yet at the same time she felt a disturbing ambivalence about Barbara's probable death. Somehow the thought of Barbara's marriage to Rowen bothered her.

"Hey, you don't have to make it sound like it was your fault," said Rowen. "It was no one's fault; it just happened."

"We'd better get moving again," Tim Fletcher advised, "before the wraith does anything else."

Leah prodded her horse back into the lead.

Gradually the forest thickened around them. The trail narrowed until it disappeared. Thorny brambles blocked the spaces between trees. Vines like snakes curled down from leafless branches and tried to entangle the horses. The moss-covered ground turned into a bog that mired down the animals.

Their progress slowed to a crawl.

When they tried to use sorcery to cut a firm path they discovered that the wood was heavily spellbound. Fighting it with magic quickly drained their energy, with little result. However, if they turned aside from the direction leading to the wraithstone, the brambles and mud soon gave way.

Stubbornly they fought forward. As the hours passed they made only a little headway. The sky darkened into a starless black lid over the unyielding forest that entombed them.

"I swear we're making less progress now than we did hours ago," said Fletcher, vainly chopping at vines with his sword.

Michael Rowen nodded. "Maybe we'd better stop and rest until daylight."

"That's fine with me." Fletcher sheathed his sword in disgust.

"I'll take first watch," said Rowen. "Then I'll transfer my stone to you, and you'll take the second. Leah will take the third."

Leah studied the small space they'd cleared for themselves and their horses. The path cut behind them remained open and inviting. The Shaltus-force surrounding them felt like a suffocating cocoon.

"Is it safe for any of us to sleep?" she asked.

Rowen shrugged. "I don't know. The closer we get to the wraithstone, the more dangerous it will be to stop and rest. The *tomaad* we've been drinking can't fully replace sleep. I think we should take this chance while we have it. There's not much use in trying to go on now anyway."

"Maybe things will be easier in the morning," Fletcher commented.

The ex-priest unsaddled his gelding, and the others

followed his example. Then they gathered old logs and broken branches for a fire. While Fletcher spread out his bedroll as far from the evil-looking bushes and vines as possible, Leah and Rowen drew rune wards on the ground. When completed, they cast a double hemisphere of protective force over the clearing. The shields glimmered faintly—one a yellow-gold aura, the other green-gold.

"Get some sleep now," Rowen told her.

"I don't know that I can." Shaltus's presence grated against her mind like a rasp.

"Tim's not having any difficulty." Rowen gestured toward the fire. Leah saw that Fletcher had curled up on his blanket and was already snoring loudly.

She smiled. "I wish I could do that, but I feel as tense as a bowstring. The wraith is waiting for us to relax our guard."

Rowen stared into the skeleton trees. Beyond their campfire it was pitch black and deathly quiet. There were no sounds of night animals; no wind rustled the plants.

"Maybe so. But you ought to at least lie down and rest." He glanced at her. "You look tired."

Leah found the concern in his eyes disturbing. Shrugging, she turned away and studied Tim Fletcher. "Some. He must really be exhausted to fall asleep so easily. This ground doesn't look very comfortable." She kicked lightly at the sorcery-hardened earth. The dirt was laced with stones, branches, twigs, and odd patches of moss and fungus.

"We're used to sleeping in the open. Compared with some of the places we've slept, this ground is a mattress. Now it's hard for us to adjust to the softness of real beds." He glanced at the cloud-shrouded sky. "I like sleeping under the stars."

"I know what you mean." Leah leaned back against one of the trees. "I've always felt more comfortable

living close to nature than inside Castle Carlton. I
guess it's because I'm half-Sylvan. But I still like the
comfort of a mattress."

Rowen smiled. "You'd like a bed outdoors, I suppose?"

"I think I would."

"The best of both worlds."

"If I could have that . . ." She frowned, suddenly
serious, thinking of her mixed blood. She'd often
wished she'd been born one thing or the other; she'd
dreamed about it, but she'd never dared dream of
acceptance on her own terms.

She quickly shifted the subject back to him. "If you
get your own kingdom, you'll have to get used to
sleeping indoors."

"There's little chance of that now, without Barbara to seal the alliance," he replied. "Perhaps it's
just as well. I'm used to this wandering life. I don't
know that I'd be happy settled in one place." He
looked across the glade at Fletcher. "Tim thinks I'd
be sick of ruling within three months, and he may
be right."

Trying not to look at Rowen's face, Leah found
herself watching his hands. His powerful fingers
twisted together nervously as he spoke.

"I thought you wanted your own kingdom?"

He sighed. "Perhaps I've wanted only a dream. As
a child I saw my father's castle destroyed in the
Great War. The lands of Rowen were transformed
into a desert. I've thought of returning there and trying to restore what was, but one sorcerer cannot
undo the destruction of hundreds.

"Sometimes, though, I remember the way my home
was, and I long to find a place like that again. But
I'd probably only discover fool's gold, not the real
thing."

"Maybe it's better to accept things the way they

are than to wonder about might-have-beens or to search for might-be's that never can be what you really want." Leah sighed. "I've spent my whole life wanting things that never could be, wishing that things had been different. It only leads to frustration and disappointment."

Rowen's fingers tapped together uncertainly. "You're probably right. I've enjoyed my life. It's been exciting, varied, challenging. I shouldn't want more."

"But you do."

"It's just that I've never had a place of my own. I don't fit anywhere."

Leah glanced up. "I know the feeling."

His slate-colored eyes met hers and held them for a moment in wordless communication.

She looked quickly away. "I'd better get some rest."

Leah felt his fingers brush her hand as she turned toward the fire. Without looking back she pulled away, crossed to the other side of the clearing, and stretched out on her bedroll.

She tried to force herself to sleep, to forget Michael Rowen, Shaltus, Quinen, her half-brother, her father, her isolation. She twisted and turned. The ground seemed made of jagged iron. The fire toasted one side of her body, while the cool, moist air chilled the other. The wraith's presence was a gnawing irritation, like the persistent itch of a mosquito bite. The more she strove to ignore it, the more aware of it she became.

Restless, she opened her eyes and watched dancing flames pirouette along the logs to the music of Fletcher's rattling snore.

Through the scarlet ballet she glimpsed Michael Rowen sitting on a tree stump by the edge of the glade. The firelight gave crimson highlights to his shoulder-length, auburn hair. His features were finely sculptured—gentle brows over large, intelligent eyes, patrician nose, full lips. Prominent cheekbones, smile lines at the corners of his eyes and mouth, and worry wrinkles across his high forehead gave his face character.

Suddenly a branch behind Rowen shifted. It became a dark, living rope that uncoiled and arched out of the tree toward his shoulders.

Leah's spell caught the diamondback in midair and flung it to the ground. Its coils contracted, twitched, relaxed, and stilled.

"What?" He was on his feet.

"Look out," shouted Leah. The trees behind him were writhing, somehow changing into other serpents.

He jerked around, ready to join his sorcery with hers.

The snakes slid through the double protective fields like worms through earth. Leah's spell had no effect on them.

"Illusion only," said Rowen calmly. "Except for this one." He kicked the dead rattler away.

"How did it get through our shields?" Leah joined him.

"It was probably here when we camped, but the wraith waited until we were more vunerable."

Leah frowned as the phantom snakes crawled closer. "Why these?"

"Perhaps to draw our attention or to cause us to waste energy trying to destroy them. Shaltus doesn't realize that my resistance to magic allows me to distinguish illusion from reality."

"Are you sure they aren't real?" asked Leah. She stepped back as a copperhead slithered toward her. It seemed far from insubstantial. The hourglass-shaped chestnut markings on its brown skin were readily distinguishable.

"It's only a projection of some sort." Rowen stepped

forward as if to kick it, but his foot passed through the phantom. "There may be some real ones among these, however." He gestured at the forest. "I'll keep an eye on them." Snakes dripped from the trees in a twisting curtain. "You'd better wake Fletcher."

Leah ran to the ex-priest. He was still in his bedroll.

As she reached to shake him, she realized that his snores had become ragged gasps.

"N'Omb's fires!" she exclaimed. His face was pale and sweaty. His eyes rolled beneath half-open lids. "I think he's been bitten," she called to Rowen.

Fletcher's brow was already fever-hot.

Something moved on the periphery of her vision. As she jerked away she heard a soft, dry rattle and felt the snake hit her leg.

She looked down and saw a long streak of blood on her trousers. The body of the rattler lay at her feet. Its severed head was a meter away—thrown there by Michael Rowen's spell when he'd seen the snake strike at her.

"Thanks."

He nodded. "Just returning the favor." He turned his attention back to the invading phantoms.

Leah probed the glade carefully with her magic. There were no more living snakes within the hemisphere of their wards.

She knelt by Fletcher and searched for the bite. It was on his right forearm. Taking his knife, she cut across the wound and sucked out as much of the venom as she could. Finally she rinsed out her mouth with *tomaad* and forced him to drink some of the Sylvan elixir. Fletcher remained semiconscious, but she guessed that he would recover.

"Leah," called Rowen. His voice was tense.

She saw pinpoints of silver flame all along the

golden shields where something small was trying to penetrate.

Touching Fletcher's forehead once more to assure herself that it was cooler, she went to Rowen. "What is it?"

"Insects, some illusion, some real."

Suddenly lightning arched out of the black sky. Bolt after bolt crashed against the wards. The cracking claps were deafening. The earth rocked, the air burned, the light dazzled.

A swarm of wasps swirled into their shields.

Leah screamed as the rune wards exploded with a force that almost knocked her down. Half-blinded by the blast, she stumbled into Rowen. His hands closed on hers. Wordlessly they united their defense, erecting a strong barrier around themselves and the still unconscious Fletcher.

Without the wards, however, it was impossible to protect the horses from the furious attack.

A jagged spear of silver illuminated the glade. Leah saw the animals clearly. They reared in fear, pulling frantically at their tethered reins. Their nostrils flared. Sweat dripped from silken coats. Their lips were stretched tightly over bared teeth. The brown-eyed mare shook. Its shriek became a shrill wail.

A bolt struck them with full force.

Leah shuddered and cried out. Nauseated, she pressed her head against Rowen's chest and tried to ignore the stench of burning flesh and bitter ozone. His hands squeezed hers comfortingly.

Then she felt a sharp burning sensation on her shoulder, like the stab of a weaver's needle. Rowen jerked away, grimacing in pain.

Some of the wasps had gotten inside their shield when the wards fell. As the lightning continued to pound them, the insects attacked with a vengeance, stinging them repeatedly. Keeping a grip on Rowen's left hand to hold their psychic link, Leah swatted the wasps with her right hand. Rowen batted at the insects with his left hand. By the time they had killed them all, their hands were swollen from the stings.

They knelt at Fletcher's side. He was fully conscious but too weak to join the link.

Throughout the night the thunderbolts continued to bombard them. Bolstered by occasional sips of *tomaad,* they had little difficulty in maintaining their united shield. They made no attempt to counterattack, however, for the wraith's power seemed inexhaustible.

At dawn the attack ceased abruptly. After the continuous barrage the sudden silence was almost painful. Leah's ears still rang with echoing thunder.

"Is it over?" she gasped, not hearing herself say the words.

"I think so." Rowen's voice seemed a whisper.

They probed the area with spells, seeking further threats, but there were none.

"The wraith will replenish its energy. Then it will attack again."

"I guess so."

"Let's get moving while we can." Rowen turned to Fletcher. "Are you feeling well enough to walk?"

"I'm all right." The ex-priest threw off his covers and rose unsteadily to his feet.

"You don't look too well." Leah studied his still-pale face and slightly shaking hands. "You'd better drink some more *tomaad.*"

"I'm just a bit woozy." Fletcher took a swig from the flask looped across his chest.

"Better take it easy on that," Rowen advised. "We don't have too much left."

Taking inventory they found that each of them still had one canteen. The rest had been destroyed along with the horses and most of their gear. They stuffed the remaining food and supplies into their bedrolls and slung them over their shoulders like packs.

Leah and Rowen set to work advancing the path. After several hours the bramble-laden swamp gave way to firmer ground and a forest of lifeless trees. Spells no longer hindered their progress. Within moments they covered more ground on foot than they had during the previous afternoon.

Leah strode forward quickly, eager to get out of the skeleton forest and into open fields. She smiled as the trees thinned. Then the grin slipped from her face as she reached the edge of the woods.

Instead of the corn fields she remembered, a vast, formal garden in full bloom lay ahead.

Inspecting it for illusion she murmured a spell, but the flowers, shrubs, statues, and fountains seemed real.

Rowen touched her arm. "What's this?"

"I don't know." She studied the rows of azaleas and roses in pink, white, and gold. There were pansies, petunias, fuchsias, goldenrod, gardenias, marigolds, orchids, and a hundred others. "This wasn't here two years ago. Is it illusion?"

"A large part seems to be real."

"A trap?"

"Maybe." Rowen looked glumly at the stylized plots of flowers and shrubs and the intertwining paths. "Which way is the wraithstone?"

Leah studied the sky. It was too overcast to see the sun, but a patch of brightness revealed its hiding place.

She pointed at the large hedges to the right. "Through the garden. Castle Bluefield would be to the left, at the foot of those dark hills. These beds seem to stretch all the way there."

"Hey . . ."

Leah jerked around. Fletcher was staring into shrubbery.

"I thought I saw someone there," he said. "I think it was a woman—but maybe I just imagined it."

"That's the direction we have to go. Let's see what we can find." Rowen headed off along a neat white pebble path. Fletcher followed quickly to stay within the aura of Rowen's protective field. Leah brought up the rear.

The walk meandered by a rock garden dotted with cactus plants. They passed topiary shrubs shaped to resemble bears, osmurs, dogs, and other animals and bronze fountains circled by nasturtiums. Beds of gladioli, goldenrod, and marigolds surrounded polished statuary that Shaltus's magic must have recently created. Rhododendrons, roses, azaleas, and evergreens edged parts of the path. There was even a tiered herbarium.

Rowen paused by a large statue of a man strangling an osmur with his bare hands.

"Notice anything strange about this?" he asked Leah.

The well-muscled figure might have been of some bronze god from an age before N'Omb's rule, for no mortal man could kill a five-meter-tall, apelike osmur. Still, there was something familiar about the man's face—his firm jaw, his cruel smile.

"Not really . . ."

"All these statues are of the same man." The sorcerer gestured toward the various marble and bronze figures ornamenting the garden. "This place is like a shrine to him."

"There's that woman again," cried Fletcher. He pointed away from the monument toward a figure fleeing along the bank of a lily-filled pond.

Unkempt raven hair hung like knotted ropes to her waist. The torn rags of a blue dress showed more of the slim figure than they concealed. A face, white and stark as a gull's wing, turned sidewise for a moment, revealing an expression of terror so great that it distorted all the features into a scream. Then she was gone, with only a trembling rose showing where she'd been.

"Barbara!" Leah whispered.

"She's still alive." Fletcher's eyes widened. "Or could she be one of Shaltus's illusions?"

"No. She's real." Rowen's brow creased into a frown. "Somehow she's still alive."

Leah started forward. "Let's go after her. She must have escaped from the wraith."

She ran ahead, with Fletcher and Rowen a few steps behind her.

A blue thread hung from a yellow rose's thorn by a branching path. She turned left. Something moved in front of her. She ran faster. A fleeting glimpse of bare arms and black hair ducking through an ivy-covered archway. She followed, cutting quickly left, right, and left again along a hedge-lined corridor.

"There she is," Fletcher called some distance behind her.

A patch of blue through the leaves.

Following closely, she shouted, "Barbara!"

"Leah?" Rowen's voice seemed far behind.

"Yes?" She turned her head, expecting to see him and Fletcher, and stopped in mid-stride. There was no one there.

"Fletcher? Rowen?"

"Here." Rowen's voice, close behind her and to the left.

She hesitated and stared at the path ahead. Barbara was tantalizingly near. But Rusty's warning not to get separated came into her mind. She turned back. The path between the thick walls of hedges forked, and she turned left, toward the sound of Rowen's voice. It forked again.

"Rowen?"

"Here." A loud cry to the left, but from the right came a weak call, like an echo. She turned left.

The path twisted and turned and came out by a large bronze fountain with a dozen lizard figures spewing forth thick sprays of water. Across from each lizard lay a path leading back into the maze, and beside each opening stood the marble figure of a man with a cold, cruel smile. It seemed to be mocking her.

Leah shivered. She *had* seen that face before, echoed in Vargo's contorted features.

"Rowen?" she called. Nothing. "Tim—Tim Fletcher?" she shouted at the top of her voice, but there was no answer.

Suddenly she felt panicky. She cupped her spellstone in her hands and sought contact with the sorcerer and the ex-priest. Her probe spun out—and met a malignant wall of force that blocked it completely.

Leah understood clearly now. The garden was a trap. Perhaps Rowen's voice had only been an illusion to draw her farther into the maze. Perhaps the others had heard the voice call to them, from the wrong direction.

She glanced at the sky. It was a uniform gray.

Taking a deep breath she turned around and began carefully retracing her steps. She turned right, then right again. Which way now? She studied the white gravel path for a footprint, the hedges for a broken branch. Nothing. She shrugged and turned left.

Cautiously she continued to search for a way out. She called for Rowen but got no answer. She tried magic and found walls of sorcery still blocking her spells. They seemed as solid and impenetrable as stone.

She was lost in the maze. Every time she tried to
retrace her steps, the path seemed to wind back to the
lizard fountain or to curve into a new corridor decorated with statues, benches, or multicolored flowers.
She broke twigs to keep from traveling in circles, but
this only seemed to lead her farther from her original
starting point.

A sudden breeze blew along the passageway. Along
with the fragrances of jasmine and lavender it carried
the soft sigh of a girl's crying.

Leah headed toward the sound. The path twisted
through several hairpin curves, passed a large, marble
statue of a lion devouring a deer, and turned into an
oval glade dominated by a falcon-shaped marble fountain that poured a sparkling stream of water into a
vase-shaped base.

"Barbara!"

Her half-sister sat on a bench in front of the font.
Although she was crying softly, her tear-streaked face
had a vacant expression without a trace of sorrow,
fear, or distress. The blue rag she wore might once
have been a nightgown, but it was too ripped and
soiled to tell. Some of the stains seemed to be dirt,
others blood. Jagged scratches, which might have
been made by fingernails or claws, ran down her arms.
The nicks on her legs and hands were more likely to
have been caused by brush or brambles.

Barbara seemed unaware of Leah's presence. While
she stared into space, her hands moved rhythmically
up and down. Repeatedly the dirt-caked fingers wove
a pattern about each other in the air. The hands fluttered like butterflies, almost as though they were
independent creatures that would fly away if they
weren't still bound to their mistress by the lifeless
arms.

It took Leah a few seconds to understand the weird
pantomime. The hands were holding an invisible flow-

er, plucking the petals off one by one, tossing the stem away, taking another flower, and repeating the process.

Leah reached toward her half-sister. Then she hesitated, fearing that she faced only a dangerous illusion. Her protective aura brightened and bubbled like molten gold.

"Barbara!" She grabbed the girl's shoulders and felt firm flesh. At the same time the sensitivity she'd always had toward her siblings confirmed the fact that this was her half-sister.

She shook Barbara roughly. Although the girl's eyes remained empty, her crying stopped with the quickness of a faucet being turned off.

Leah pulled her sister to her feet, studied her vacant stare, and then slapped her face.

Barbara's brown eyes fluttered, focused, and widened as fear flooded into the blankness. She twisted in Leah's arms like a terror-stricken doe bolting from a hunter.

Leah held on and pulled the smaller girl around toward her. "Barbara. Barbara. It's Leah. I won't hurt you."

Recognition glimmered through the madness and fear in the fawn-colored eyes. Barbara stopped squirming. Her face was as tight as the skin of a drum. "Leah?"

"Yes." Carefully Leah released her sister from the none-too-gentle embrace.

Barbara's eyes darted from side to side, looking suspiciously around the glade. "He's not just tricking me?" Her pale face was filled with confusion.

"I'm real, not one of Shaltus's illusions," Leah answered, certain that Barbara was referring to the wraith. "How did you get away from him?"

"Ran. Ran." The girl's hands pulled frantically at each other.

Leah gently reached for her. Barbara jerked away, spun into a half-crouch, and fearfully wrapped her arms around herself.

"It's all right. We'll find our way out of here." Leah stretched out her arm. "Come with me."

"Out?"

"Out." She took one of Barbara's twitching hands and caressed it gently between her own. "You'll be safe. Come."

The smaller girl rose and followed Leah with uncertain steps toward one of the three paths leading from the fountain. Suddenly she sobbed and tugged urgently at Leah's arm.

"No. No. No."

"Not that way?" asked Leah curiously.

"He's . . . he's there." Barbara's fingers entwined themselves around Leah's wrist like snakes. They tugged her toward the second path, directly opposite the one that had led Leah to the fountain.

"Out. Out." The note of urgency in Barbara's voice bordered on hysteria.

"All right," said Leah calmly. She sensed that Barbara was unstable, on the edge of madness or perhaps already over the brink. Anything might trigger her into flight.

Holding her sister's hand tightly, Leah expanded her protective aura around the girl. Then she led her half-sister into the hedge-lined corridor.

Although Barbara's fingers continued to twist animatedly, her face relaxed into a vacant stare. She followed Leah docilely.

The path curved in on itself and then out and out. It was obviously heading to the periphery of the maze. An archway appeared in the wall of leaves. It was an exit identical to the entrance.

"N'Omb be praised," sighed Leah, ducking through.

She'd begun to think she'd be trapped forever in the labyrinth.

She pulled up short on the other side to stare ahead in shocked silence at the bright-hued garden running down to the steps of Castle Bluefield where several Sylvan stood as though they'd been waiting for her. Among them was Quinen. His expression changed from satisfaction to surprise to troubled dismay as he saw her.

Before Leah could move, Barbara's fingers twisted suddenly and slipped from her grip. Her half-sister's hands knotted together and crashed like a rock into the top of Leah's head.

Thirteen

"Tie her tightly now. Very tightly."

The rich contralto edging into Leah's consciousness was hauntingly familiar, yet totally alien—Barbara's voice, twisted and corrupted by the exultant menace of the wraith.

Ignoring the throbbing ache at the back of her head, Leah blinked and forced her eyes open.

Two young Sylvan warriors were tying her hands behind her back. Her pack and the precious flask of *tomaad* had been cast aside.

Nearby stood Quinen. His unpainted face was expressionless, but his silver and topaz eyes seemed shadowed with guilt. Beyond him stood Barbara.

Or rather what had once been Barbara.

Leah had seen this face in marble—now the features were carved in flesh. The lips were a firm, cruel line. The hard jaw jutted out farther than it should have. The pale skin was as tight and smooth as a mask; yet the whole face had aged.

Around Barbara's neck hung Leah's powerstone.

Frantically Leah tried to contact the stone with her mind, even though she knew it would do her no good. She could not control the stone if it were farther than a hand's length from her body. Without the spellstone for amplification, her psychic powers were too weak to do more than hold a leaf in midair or light a match.

"Bring her to the castle," said the wraith-possessed

girl in a too-deep contralto. It made Leah's flesh crawl.

Then the image of Shaltus melted from Barbara's features like liquid wax, leaving an empty pool, void of emotion or personality.

Twitching in a puppet's dance, Barbara marched off to the fortress.

Leah shuddred. She tried to suppress the horror she felt more for herself than for her half-sister. How long would it take for the wraith to turn her into a lurching automaton?

The Sylvan stood. They had finished their task.

Leah tested the bonds. The rope was strong and tight enough to cut her flesh as she twisted against it.

Measuring the distance to the tall hedges marking the boundary of the maze, she sized up her chance of getting to her feet and into the greenery. It was no good. If they couldn't outrun her, the Sylvan could have the plants hold her.

Quinen waved his soldiers off. "I want to talk to her for a moment," he told them.

He reached down and pulled her to her feet.

"I am truly sorry to see you here, Leahdes. I thought you were smart enough to stay away from this place. I figured that you must have warned Rowen of our ambush, but it never crossed my mind that you'd accompany him here."

She answered nonchalantly, hiding her fear. "When I saw your reception party I thought you were expecting me."

"The wraith stationed us here to catch any game flushed from its trap. I was expecting Rowen. Where is he?"

"Ask the wraith." Her smile was honey laced with hemlock.

"No matter. We'll snare him soon enough." He avoided her gaze. "I am sorry you're here."

"As sorry as you were to kill Trask?"

His hands clenched. "How did you find out about that anyway?"

"A bit of human magic . . . ," she taunted.

Studying her face he frowned, and his voice softened. "I didn't want to hurt Trask, but he found out I was an Expansionist. I don't want to see you hurt either, but I have no choice." He gripped her arm tightly and swung her around toward the castle. "Shaltus is waiting for you."

Leah pressed herself against his chest and stared earnestly into his eyes.

"Break your pact with the wraith now, before it's too late. Shaltus is just using you, can't you see that? It will destroy you when it has what it wants."

"It uses me, and I use it. I can control it."

"Can you? It's of human sorcery, not Sylvan. If you could not detect my simple spell, what makes you think you can stop its awesome power?"

Doubt flickered across his face. Then he spun her roughly away.

"No. It will die when all the S'Carltons do." He gestured toward the castle. "It's time for you to go in."

She searched his face, trying to think of another way she could appeal to him, but the doubt and guilt in his eyes had vanished into a sea of ice. He took her arm and led her toward the castle.

All but one of the other Sylvan returned to their positions guarding the exit to the maze. The remaining man moved to Leah's left side as a second escort.

"I am sorry," Quinen repeated.

"I'm sorry for you," Leah replied. There was nothing else to say.

They entered the castle.

It looked to Leah as though a century had passed since she'd been there last, though it had only been a little more than two years. She remembered that day well—the day the Shaltus-wraith killed her father.

The massive iron door leading into the inner court-yard was torn off its hinges. It looked like a crumpled fan that had been tossed aside by some giant. Although no damage had been apparent from the outside, the inner wall of the Clock Tower was ripped away and piled into a mound of rubble in the center of the yard. Broken floors jutted from the outer wall; the roof had collapsed; the spiral staircase had melted into a pile of slag.

A pit gaped where the small N'Omb chapel used to be. The forebuilding to the keep seemed to have been gutted by fire. Only the exterior stones of the keep itself were unbroken.

Inside, the walls glistened with slime. The carpet was a rotting mass of corruption. Velvet drapes hung in crimson tatters. Once-beautiful tapestries dripped from the walls like fungus. Ornamental gold leaf peeled from the ceilings, and plaster oozed like pus.

The air stank of decay. A thick gray paste of dust coated the wooden floor. Cobwebs hung across side corridors and empty doorways like drapes.

They led her through the Hall of Mirrors, up the staircase, and into the Great Hall.

The overstuffed couches with silken covers that had lined the walls were gone. So was the great oak table. A few of its ornately carved chairs remained, broken and tossed like firewood into a pile near the stair.

Roaring with scarlet flames that had no apparent fuel, the hearth cast strange shadows across barren walls and lofty windows with finely carved paneling and tracery, to the graceful three-sided oriel at the other end of the hall. The alcove by the bay window held several life-sized statues of Shaltus.

A rack dominated the room. Bloodstains spotted its wood. Other instruments of torture, glinting coldly in the half-light, lay on a nearby table.

Several figures huddled against the far wall: Barbara, with unseeing eyes and weaving hands that plucked invisible petals from a nonexistent flower; a scarecrow-thin giant with half his face gone, apparently eaten away, who played with a rat; and a deformed man whose twisted arms bent unnaturally, as though they had extra joints. The last had a crooked foot, an oddly jutting hip, a broken nose, and an almost-bald head. He was a missing tradesman whom Leah had last seen straight, whole, and thick-haired.

Terror ripped through her, but her face remained granite-hewed. Her hands trembled. Salty sweat burned wrists rubbed raw against their bonds.

She stared at her spellstone. It still hung around Barbara's neck like a worthless trinket. If the wraith had left the stone in plain view to torment her, it had succeeded. It was frustrating to know the stone was so close, yet utterly useless. Barbara was as oblivious to the stone as to the world around her. She was hopelessly insane, ensorcelled, or both. And even if she hadn't been, it would have done no good, for she had neither the training nor the talent to use the gem.

Abruptly, gloating laughter filled the room. The sound was as dark as night, as cold as frost, as deep as a grave.

In front of the fire stood a shadow-shape that seemed to pull darkness from the corners of the room, piling shadow on shadow, building into the phantom shape of a man.

Its face was a dark image of the ones carved in marble across the hall, its smile a cruel slash.

The wraith moved toward them. Its specter-body flowed like mist, yet somehow maintained the illusion of life, seeming to walk, talk, and breathe like a mortal man.

"Your father must be repaid the debt of my death," it said. "You shall suffer as I did."

The wraith reached out toward Leah. Quinen drew

back an arm's length behind her, and the Sylvan guard backstepped to the door as quickly as possible.

Shaltus's fingers were icicles that numbed as they passed through her arm and seared as they withdrew. It stepped away, leaving her arm throbbing with excruciating pain. Yet Leah sensed that all the *tomaad* she'd drunk lessened the effect. She could still move her fingers.

"Put her on the rack," the wraith ordered Quinen. "Then get out." The voice cracked through the air like a whip, sending the second Sylvan bolting out the door.

Quinen's back stiffened. His hand tightened around Leah's arm, but he made no move toward the torture frame.

"Is this necessary? Can't you give her a quick death?" he protested.

"You question me?" roared the wraith.

The giant and the tradesman jerked upright, their eyes soulless.

They ran forward, pulled Leah from Quinen's grasp, and took her to the rack. She struggled and kicked at them, but she couldn't free herself. Both seemed inhumanly strong. Their hands were iron claws that bound her, spread-eagled, on the table.

The tall Sylvan still faced the wraith. His face reddened angrily, but he said nothing.

"I shall enjoy her pain." Shaltus's voice was a menacing rasp.

His shadow-eyes appraised Quinen with cold calculation. "She is a beautiful woman—you might like to have her." His smile became a leer.

The giant smirked and the merchant grinned.

Trembling uncontrollably, Leah strained against the unyielding ropes.

Quinen grimaced. "No!"

"No?" The wraith seemed amused. "It's easy."

He pointed at Barbara. The girl came alive. Her lips curved into a sensuous smile as she spun into a wanton dance.

"Her sister was very nice," chuckled Shaltus.

Barbara threw herself against Quinen, kissed him, and ran her hands over his body. Taunting and teasing him, she whirled away.

The giant ran to her. They circled one another in a sinuous dance that became an obscene caricature of lovemaking.

Leah tried to turn away, to close her eyes, heart, and mind to what was happening, but the Shaltus-force jerked her head back and made her watch.

"I can control her or not," said the wraith with a sly look at Quinen, "as it pleases you."

It gestured toward Barbara. Suddenly her attitude changed from willingness to resistance. Wild horror replaced the blank look on her face. She whimpered like a terrified child.

The merchant and the giant grabbed her arms and pulled her to the floor. Clawing at them, Barbara tried to crawl away, but they held her fast.

Then one of the statues of Shaltus in the back of the room quivered and began to move. The marble gleamed like mother of pearl in the darkness. The sculpture lurched off its base, the stone groaned and shifted, and it awkwardly walked forward with thudding steps.

Barbara saw the animated statue and screamed. Her eyes held madness and dread.

The life-sized sculpture reached her.

Leah cried out as she suddenly realized what the statue was going to do. She gasped with nausea, but the wraith's power would not even allow her that release. She shuddered with dry heaves as the wraith forced her to watch.

Quinen was also rooted in place, helpless even to avert his eyes.

The wraith's laughter was a deep, sensuous exultation.

When the stone creature finished with Barbara, it rose and shuffled toward the rack.

"Now it's your turn," said the wraith.

"Barbara, my spellstone!" cried Leah. Her eyes fastened desperately on the amber pendant as she struggled helplessly. But Barbara lay twitching on the floor. Her face was contorted in madness, her hands again weaving through the air plucking nonexistent petals.

"No!" shouted Quinen. He moved into the statue's path. "She's a Sylvan. Our bargain never included her in the first place, and it certainly never included this horror."

The marble beast froze in its steps.

The wraith laughed.

"Bargain? You stupid tree-eater—did you really think I'd keep any pact with the likes of you? I know what you've been thinking. You thought you'd help me and then be rid of me when I had destroyed the S'Carltons and their kingdom."

It laughed again, and the sound raked across Leah's skull like a steel rasp against bone.

"But that won't happen. As each one dies I'll just get stronger, and when they're dead, I will control Carlton, not you."

The statue lurched forward again, heading for Leah.

"What have I done?" Quinen murmured in horror. His face purpled with rage and shame.

Then he used his Sylvan powers. Transforming and shaping the wooden floor, he changed the area beneath the sculpture into mush. The statue toppled.

The wood solidified once more, immobilizing the stone.

The giant and the balding merchant rushed toward Quinen. Suddenly the wooden floor seemed to liquify. It exuded branchlike arms that entwined around the men's legs, pulling them down. The limbs lengthened into vine-sized tendrils. They tightened around the men like ropes. Several became strangling nooses around their throats.

The men struggled frantically. Terror now filled their once vacant eyes.

Watching them and the now smiling wraith-specter, Leah sensed that Shaltus had released his control and was enjoying seeing them suffer.

As the two men strangled and died, Quinen turned toward Leah. The hemp-made rope binding her wrists and ankles twisted spasmodically, jerked, and began to unravel.

Laughing, the wraith gestured at Quinen. A jagged bolt of force arced from its shadow-hand into the large Sylvan and hurled him across the room. Quinen smashed into a wall and lay still.

With all her strength Leah strained against the frayed ropes, snapping them.

She lunged toward Barbara. Her spellstone swung loosely from her half-sister's throat.

As Leah flung herself at the stone, the wraith's power coiled around her, pulling her aside. She hit the floor and was frozen into immobility centimeters from her half-sister, but still too far from the stone.

Barbara rose and danced away.

A second statue groaned as it came alive.

Unable to move, Leah could only stare in horror as it advanced toward her.

The door burst open.

Fourteen

The phantom shape of Shaltus swirled into a dark cloud of force that vaulted across the room. It descended on the figures that entered—Michael Rowen and Timothy Fletcher.

At that moment the statue halted in midstride as it returned to solid stone, the fire whooshed out, and Barbara collapsed near the wall.

The force holding Leah diminished slightly as the wraith turned its attack on the two men. Although she was now able to move a little, every time she tried to stand or crawl the force tightened around her again like a python's coils, preventing her from reaching her half-sister.

Lightning struck within the cloud, but failed to pierce the men's shield. Thunder echoed across the hall.

The two figures separated. Michael Rowen stepped through the protective aura, passed through the wraith's field of shadows and power, and ran across the room. Leah was surprised to see that he no longer wore his spellstone. Then she remembered his immunity to magic. Staring at the funneling shadows that still held Fletcher, she realized that the ex-priest remained within a green-gold shield. Evidently Rowen had transferred his spellstone to Fletcher before they'd entered the castle.

The tall sorcerer reached Leah and tried to help her up, but she was not immune to Shaltus's force and remained pinned to the ground.

She fought the paralysis that froze her throat when she tried to speak.

"What?" asked Rowen, seeing her lips try to move.

She turned her arm slightly and gestured with her fingers toward the spot on her chest where her spell-stone normally hung. Then she crooked her fingers toward Barbara.

"Your stone. Of course. Where?" Rowen looked around. Puzzled, he followed her gaze, took a few hesitant steps in that direction, and then headed determinedly toward Barbara.

The sound of stone grinding against wood made Leah's head jerk up. She stared in horror at the shape coming to life behind Rowen. She tried to yell, to scream, to warn him, but no sound could escape from her lips.

The statue's marble arms reached for the sorcerer.

But Barbara's eyes snapped open. Rowen saw their terror. He turned and managed to avoid the stone-strong fingers. He drew his sword and slashed at the creature. The sword broke against the rock.

Rowen dodged back. The clumsy automaton followed slowly.

The tall sorcerer reached Barbara, pulled the spell-stone from her neck, and tossed it toward Leah.

The statue grabbed him.

As the gem sailed through the air, Leah concentrated on it. It fell too far to the left. Desperately she forced her reluctant arms toward it. Then the chain was within her grasp.

The Shaltus-sculpture dissolved into rubble as her spell hit it. Her aura flashed around her body to block the paralysis. She ran to Rowen.

His left arm hung uselessly at his side, apparently broken, but otherwise he was unhurt.

"Let's get out of here," he shouted.

Leah reached for her half-sister and pulled the trembling girl upright. Her mind was still entombed in an incoherent terror from which it might never escape.

"She's insane," said Leah softly. "We must take her with us. We can't let Shaltus touch her again."

She covered her half-sister with her shield, but this time she took the precaution of binding the girl with a spell so that she could not be used as Shaltus's mindless tool.

Now the wraith hurled lightning at Leah and Rowen, while continuing its attack against the cloud-trapped ex-priest.

Linking hands, Leah and Rowen ran to Fletcher's aid. Barbara followed meekly under Leah's control.

Numbing cold hit as they attempted to enter the funnel-shaped shadows encircling Fletcher. Rowen seemed unaffected, but both Barbara and Leah shivered. Shafts of lightning expanded into engulfing sheets of flame. Barbara twitched as Shaltus attempted to reassert his control over her, but Leah's spell was strong enough to block his influence.

Wincing in pain, Rowen reached with his broken arm through the thunder and mist to take Fletcher's hand. The slender ex-priest's face was tense with fatigue and strain. As their fingers touched the men united their spells with Leah's. The three counterattacked as one.

The vortex of shadows and storm whirled around them frantically, seeking any weakness in their combined shields. Then the darkness faded. The lightning flashed sporadically. The black cloud split apart and dissipated. The air stilled. Apparently the wraith had expended a great deal of energy in controlling all the humans and in the series of attacks. It was weakening.

"Let's get out now," ordered Rowen. He released Leah's and Fletcher's hands.

Leah took her half-sister's arm and followed as the two men ran toward the large double doors leading out of the Great Hall. Scattered thunderbolts pursued them.

In the flashing light Leah noticed Quinen's body against the wall. She froze. His boyish face was death-still.

Distressed, she looked quickly away. She didn't want to feel sad and regretful; she didn't want to feel anything. Yet those emotions were there, along with a contradictory bitterness and resentment that left her uncertain of just how sorry she was to see him dead.

Even though he'd aided the wraith, Quinen had not really wanted to see her hurt, and in the end he'd died trying to help her. If things had only been different, she thought wistfully, perhaps if she hadn't been a half-breed . . . But she'd spent all her life wondering about might-have-beens—maybe it was time for her to accept realities.

"Leah, let's go." Rowen was beside her. "Come on." He touched her arm and gestured at the door that Fletcher held open.

Nodding, Leah prodded Barbara forward.

She didn't look back as she followed him into the hall.

Inside the corridor they moved sluggishly through foul air as thick and slimy as wet dough. It clung to their faces, making them choke and struggle for breath. The walls, floor, and ceiling seemed distorted into shimmering curves that rippled like water.

A bookcase rocked on its base and crashed to the floor, almost hitting Rowen. A suit of armor stumbled out of a crossing hallway and blocked their path until

Fletcher's spell knocked it into a gleaming pile of metal.

They reached the stairwell. When they began to descend, the stone steps suddenly altered shape to become a chute. It sent them falling, sliding, and spinning to a floor studded with knife-sharp jags of rock that would have stabbed them if Leah and Fletcher hadn't been shielding the group. Even so, the fall was bruising, and Rowen's already broken arm splintered again.

"We must heal it," said Leah, staring in dismay at the tip of bone protruding through his forearm. Lines of pain etched Rowen's face.

Fletcher rushed to Rowen and made him drink some *tomaad*.

"Magic's no help to him," he reminded Leah. "He's immune; but this Sylvan stuff may do some good. You'd better have some too." He passed the canteen to Leah when Rowen finished.

"It's almost empty."

"Finish it. This one's about half-full." The ex-priest tapped the canteen strapped across his chest.

"You shouldn't have come after me," said Leah. "You should have gone on to Shaltus's spellstone."

"No." Pain edged Rowen's voice. "I couldn't leave you. We're a team." The sincerity in his steel gray eyes disconcerted Leah.

"I'll splint that arm," said Fletcher. He drew his sword, removed the scabbard from his belt, and began ripping his shirt into strips. Then he set the bone and used the scabbard as a splint. The *tomaad's* restorative powers kept Rowen conscious throughout the ordeal.

Shadows began to gather around them.

"Hurry," cried Leah, fearing another attack.

Fletcher tied a wide piece of torn cloth around Michael Rowen's shoulder as a sling. Then he picked

up his unsheathed blade, extended it before him, and
led the way down the hall.

They entered into a long, mirrored corridor studded
with doorways. Shadows hung like mist upon the air.
Distorted reflections of themselves mimicked their
movements. The images changed, forming grotesque
shapes.

Paper-thin reflections danced in the glass. They
shifted into headless caricatures that hardly seemed
human. Rippling faces suddenly leered out of the next
pane; then the misshapen features whirled in the glass,
and elongated heads dangled from inverted bodies.

As the reflections abruptly flipped back up, a man's
shape loomed behind Leah's image. Wizened face,
emaciated body, flowing white beard and hair were
outlined against the shadows at the end of the corridor.

She turned. No one was there.

Layers of shadows formed a pool of darkness where
they had entered the hall. The face had not been
Shaltus's; yet it had been disturbingly familiar. Determinedly Leah looked away from the distorted images
in the glass, grabbed Barbara's arm, and hurried the
girl after the two men.

Cloth rustled behind her. Leather brushed against
the stone floor.

She spun around.

He stood near one of the doorways a few paces
away. His clothes were rags, his face was too thin, his
bearing was that of a stoop-shouldered old man, but
Leah knew him.

"Father?" she whispered. It had to be an illusion.
He couldn't still be alive. Although she'd never seen
his body, she'd sensed his death at the end of his duel
with Shaltus.

The gaunt figure crooked his fingers, gesturing her
to follow. Then he disappeared through the doorway.

A hand touched her shoulder. Startled, she jerked away.

"Oh, Rowen."

"What is it?"

"I thought I saw someone following us. He . . . he went in there." She pointed at the dark opening. "I think it was, it may have been . . ." She hesitated, not wanting to say it, as if telling what she'd seen would confirm its reality somehow.

"Who?" He studied her with concern.

"It might have been . . . my father."

"It must have been an illusion. The wraith would not have let your father live so long."

"Of course, it must have been an illusion."

"Come on now." He took her hand and led her back toward Fletcher.

Had she seen only a wraith-controlled specter? Leah desperately wanted to believe that. Yet she couldn't help thinking that Shaltus had only tortured Barbara, instead of killing her outright. Was it possible her father was still alive?

The thought gnawed at her as they wound their way through shadow-twisted corridors to the keep's entryway.

They halted in front of the heavy oak door leading out to the courtyard. It was closed and locked.

"I'll get it," said Fletcher. Rowen's spellstone still hung around his neck. The ex-priest cupped it in his hands, pressed the stone against the lock, and began reciting a spell.

Although Leah had gotten used to the castle's odor of decay, a sudden breeze behind her brought her head around. She sniffed in dismay at the pungent odor of corruption. Then she jumped back in alarm.

A scarecrow figure lunged out of the shadows. Eyes that might have belonged to her father stared vacantly at her. Gnarled hands brought up a sword.

The blade crashed downward. It hit the aura of her shield, bounced off, and came at her again. This time the blade shimmered unnaturally. It turned translucent and cut through her protective field like a knife through cheese.

Even though Leah realized that the weapon was not a true sword, only something made of magic and illusion, the sight of her father's face kept her from reacting quickly enough to counter it.

The blade touched her shoulder. It seared her skin as she backed away, seeming more like fire than cold steel.

Then Michael Rowen was beside her. He shouted and tackled the specter. His good arm passed through the thing's body as though it were made of air. He clutched at something substantial inside its "chest" and twisted at what he held.

Shaltus's laugh echoed over the hall. It was cavern-cold and hollow.

The image of Leah's father rippled like a disturbed reflection in water. It vanished. In its place stood a skeleton shape of rotting flesh, ragged cloth, and bone. Empty eye sockets stared out of a shrunken skin-covered skull that seemed more of a grotesque mask than what was left of the face that had belonged to a Lord of Carlton.

Leah screamed.

Long-dead hands dripping flesh and foulness tightened around Rowen's throat.

Fletcher shouted, hurling a spell at the thing. Its bones snapped apart.

Gagging, Leah looked away as arms, legs, ribs, and head collapsed into a decomposing mass on the floor. She staggered to the wall and leaned against it for support.

"Are you all right?" asked Rowen. He moved cautiously away from the crumpled skeleton.

Leah forced her head up and nodded.

Clenching her spellstone tightly in her right hand, she turned toward the disintegrating remains. She murmured a spell. Rags, bones, and flesh turned to dust. The wraith would not be able to reanimate them again.

"I've got the door open," said Tim Fletcher.

Leah grabbed Barbara's arm as they followed the ex-priest through the courtyard.

Outside the castle walls lay the crumpled bodies of three Sylvan.

"What happened to them?" asked Leah.

"We saw them on the way in and managed to surprise them," explained Fletcher. "I guess Shaltus was preoccupied with you at the time and didn't notice us until we entered the castle." He gestured toward the formal gardens behind the fortress. "They've left several horses over there."

Suddenly Fletcher's eyes widened in surprise. Leah followed his gaze. There were large gaps in the neatly arranged flower beds. The gaps increased in frequency farther from the fortress.

"The garden was partly illusion," said Rowen. "Evidently the wraith is weakening. It has only been harassing us since we left the great chamber."

Leah shrugged. "It may be conserving its strength, but its power is enormous. And it will grow stronger as we near the central spellstone."

"Then we'd better get going before it can replenish itself."

With her half-sister in tow Leah followed the men into the garden.

They found five Sylvan horses tethered by an enormous bronze statue of Shaltus. Shuddering, Leah looked away from the cruel features. Everything had happened too quickly, but now reaction was beginning to set in. Her whole body seemed jangled and tense.

Rowen and Fletcher each took a horse, while Leah and Barbara sat together on the third. They released the others.

The Sylvan saddlebags contained a still-fresh supply of *delaap* nuts and some small flasks of *tomaad*, so they ate a hurried meal as they rode through the garden.

Lightning cracked the sky. Clouds that had been fluffy cumulus pillows swirled together, lowered, and darkened. In moments a torrential rain swept across the ground. The paths became muddy streams. Fierce hail slammed into them. Lightning struck the earth repeatedly.

At the same time phantom shapes of air and magic lunged at the horses unexpectedly, making them rear and bolt. Fletcher's mount twisted crazily, nearly throwing him. Leah had to use her Sylvan powers to control the animals.

Dark pits, like shallow graves, appeared in the path ahead. The horses swerved into the flower beds. Rose thorns raked their legs.

Numbing terror pounded their minds as it had when they'd first entered Shaltus's territory. Lightning flashed faster. It seemed to light the sky continuously.

Without *tomaad* to replenish the energy they'd spent fighting the wraith they would have been lost.

Leah spotted a white marble pavilion silhouetted against the rain-drenched sky on the crest of the next hill, a little more than a kilometer away.

She pointed it out to the others. "I believe the spellstone of Shaltus is there," she shouted. The incessant thunder almost drowned her words.

"We'll never make it," cried Fletcher. His face was pale with strain and fatigue.

Lightning hit him directly, flaring outward in a brilliant white nimbus as his shield absorbed and reflected the blow. His spell deflected a second and a third bolt, diverting them into a nearby fountain. As they hit they blew the marble and bronze apart. Water sizzled, sparks cascaded across the ground, and the air crackled.

Leah felt her control of the horses begin to slip. Their minds were numb with fear that was requiring more and more effort to block. Barbara had sagged forward, faint from exhaustion, terror, or both.

Leah glanced up to find Rowen's gray eyes regarding her with concern. He seemed tired, and he must have been in agony, but his immunity to magic at least protected him from the Shaltus-induced fear that tried to paralyze Leah and Fletcher.

"I think it's time for us to separate," said the sorcerer.

Fletcher nodded. "Here's the device." He removed a large leather bag looped through his belt. "The fuse is ready to go. Light it, and then get as far away as you can as fast as you can. You'll only have a few seconds. Do you have the matches I gave you?"

"Yes."

Leah stared curiously at the bag. She wondered what sort of weapon was inside. Where had Tim Fletcher gotten the ancient magic powder that would activate it?

Silently she said a prayer to N'Omb, asking for forgiveness for her part in using the forbidden thing. Yet at the same time she prayed that N'Omb would bless the device and make it work. She did not want to think about what would happen if it did not.

"Don't let the powder get wet," advised Fletcher. "The pipe is wrapped in oilskin, so it should be dry; you'll have to keep it that way when you take it out."

"All right."

"Are you sure you know what to do?"

"I'm sure." Rowen studied the raging storm and the pattern of flowers, statues, and vanished gardens that led to the gazebo. "After I've gone, hit the structure with everything you've got. That will have to do as our diversion."

"Will you be able to make it without our shields?" asked Leah.

Rowen's forehead creased; then his lips curved upward in a wry smile. "I hope so."

He dismounted and handed his reins to Fletcher. "There's no use taking the horse; it has no immunity."

The ex-priest clasped the sorcerer's shoulder. "Good luck."

"Be careful," Leah whispered.

Michael Rowen slipped out of Fletcher's protective aura and ran down the hillside. Leah watched worriedly as he disappeared into the shrubbery. The wraith took no action against him. She wondered if his immunity to the effects of magic also protected him from its detection.

"Let's go," yelled Fletcher.

Urging their horses in the direction of the next hill they began a united spell. Their auras formed a double circle of force over the horses. It filtered out some of the fear that Shaltus still directed at them.

What remained was a baseless, debilitating terror that tried to cloud their thinking.

Fletcher signaled toward the marble pavilion. Together they blasted it with a spell that half-melted the roof but left the marble columns and base undamaged.

Suddenly the marble glowed. It shimmered and shifted. When the light died out the roof had been restored to an untouched stone dome.

Laughter mocked them. Shadows swirled out of thin air. They caked against the double circle of shields.

A psychic probe rammed through the auras like a sharp steel spike. Leah pushed it away, but not before she felt Shaltus's presence touch her mind. Its malice lingered, staining her thoughts.

Fletcher's face was ashen.

The throbbing thunder became Shaltus's voice, laughing at them. "An unfrocked priest and a half-breed fighting me! What fools you are! If the High Lord of Carlton could not destroy me, what makes you think you can?"

The air around them bubbled and popped like boiling lava. Waves of fear pounded against the shields and trickled through like water filtering through sand.

Leah's head throbbed with pain. She tried to block the terror and the other false emotions that flooded in with it—sadness, shame, and almost unbearable loneliness.

"Priest! So you call yourself a priest. But your friends called you a traitor, didn't they?" Shaltus's laughter was the roar of the ocean against granite cliffs.

Sweat beaded Fletcher's forehead. The false emotions were strengthening the effect of the insults. He squeezed Leah's hand, recited another spell, and tried to ignore the wraith.

Leah and Fletcher aimed beams of force against the gazebo. Flames crowned its domed roof without effect.

"They kicked you out. They spit on your ideas, didn't they?" the wraith hissed. "You failed your friends, you failed your god, you failed yourself."

Fletcher's hand shook within Leah's. She gripped it more tightly.

Golden spears of lightning streaked out of the dark clouds. As they countered the bolts some were deflected, while others exploded above them into sparkling light-shards. The attack continued with unrelenting ferocity, until they could not stop all of the blows.

Lightning began to hit them.

Leah's skin tingled, and her hair stood on end. While her shield continued to absorb the force adequately, Fletcher's began to fade into a red-and-brown aura as it failed.

"Fight it," yelled Leah. "Don't let it get to you."

The ex-priest pulled up his flask of *tomaad* and took a long sip. He swayed in his saddle. His face was moon-white. Then his shield turned pink and orange as it stabilized on a weaker level.

Leah hurled energy at the gazebo. As the silver shafts burst harmlessly against the marble, she caught sight of Rowen near the base. The wraith had evidently become aware of his presence. It was using a shadow-cloud of sorcery against him. The shadows spun around Rowen like a swarm of angry bees, but did not harm him.

"And a half-breed, a Sylvie bitch . . ." The wraith's voice jerked her upright. "Are you a whore like your mother?"

Leah's face reddened. Fear and shame flooded her senses, throwing her off balance. She knew that the wraith was behind the emotions, trying to break her concentration. She tried to close her mind to its insults and to the false emotions that pricked at her thoughts; it was not so easy to ignore the real emotions that they stirred inside.

She willed herself back in control and continued her attack on the gazebo. However, her spells still bounced off the marble monument without effect.

"Are you a tree-eater like her? Or a tree-lover like your father?"

She threw another spell at the gazebo's roof. Michael Rowen had reached its steps. The dome trembled slightly as she watched the tall sorcerer slip inside.

"You are as stupid and weak as S'Carlton was. I destroyed him, and I will destroy you." Shaltus chuckled. His laugh became the wind's roar as it whirled into a funnel-shaped cloud around them.

Made more of sorcery than wind, the tornado enveloped them in streamers of light that exploded into multicolored bursts of force. Clouds of vapor boiled through the air outside their shields. The wraith tried to blast apart the barriers.

Abruptly Fletcher's shield collapsed in a shower of sparks.

Leah's aura shuddered under the full force of the wraith's attack. The world spun around her. Bands of fire cut into her skull. Somehow she held the shield in place.

She was aware of Fletcher's hand still inside hers and of a weak trickle of power from him. She was surprised that he was still conscious.

The burning in her head spread down over her body. Formless terror wrapped her in numbing fear.

"Give up, tree-eater. Why prolong your pain?"

"No!" she cried stubbornly.

Energy seemed to be leaking out of her shield faster than she could channel it in.

What was taking Rowen so long? She had to continue to distract the wraith somehow.

The memory of Rusty's voice echoed through her mind—"It will use your weaknesses against you. You must use its weakness against it."

She shouted at the wind and shadows. "I may be a half-breed, but at least I'm alive. You are nothing more than a whisper of thought trapped in rock."

Lightning hit and exploded against her shield, spewing out jagged bursts of light and flames that crackled along the edge of her aura.

"You cannot destroy me so easily," she called haughtily, hiding fear and fatigue. She knew she could not take much more. "I'm of S'Carlton's blood, and he is the one who killed the man Shaltus. But you are not Shaltus." Shadows like talons scratched restlessly against her shield. "There is nothing of him left but an echo. And even echoes eventually die."

"Is this an echo?" laughed the Shaltus-wraith as the tornado whirled up again with deafening force.

The ground shook. The air roared. Only the thin golden haze protected Leah, Fletcher, Barbara, and the horses from annihilation.

The aura began to fade. It turned orange, then pink.

In a last desperate effort Leah diverted some of her power from the shield into an illusion. Her aura dimmed further, to a dangerously weak brown.

In front of the horses stood the illusion of a castle wall. A silver cage hung from the battlement. Inside was a man.

The man smiled cruelly as he looked away from the taunting crowd below him. The cage fit him like a glove, forcing him to stand. Open sores, bruises, and marks of a lash showed where he'd been tortured.

Then the illusion altered. The man seemed to pale. The arms chained above his head were thinner. A light growth of beard was beginning to cover his firm jaw. His features twisted in torment. He opened his mouth to scream, but his voice, hoarse from hours of screaming, was a dry rasp.

The wind howled. Shadows pounded frantically against Leah's shield.

The image changed again. The man hung limply inside the cage. Flies buzzed around his head. The corpse grew bloated. Pus oozed out of the flesh. Then the flesh began to rot away until bones peeked out of the corruption.

Something that was part lightning and storm, part shadow and magic, part whirlwind and night smashed into the illusion and ripped it apart. Then it hit Leah's shield.

Just as Leah's shield failed altogether, an explosion

went off inside the pavilion. The Shaltus-force surrounding her shattered into a thousand shadows, which disintegrated and vanished.

White light and flame flared through the marble pillars. One of the columns rocked, cracked, and fell. The rest of the building shook, then settled back into place.

Stunned and disoriented, Leah waited for Shaltus's next blow. Then she realized that Michael Rowen had blown up the wraithstone.

Leaves, branches, dirt, and rocks, hurled into the air by the explosion, fell to the earth in a black rain. The unnatural clouds dissipated, revealing dusk-darkened purple sky.

The silence now seemed as strange as the roaring wind had been.

"It's dead," murmured Fletcher. "Gone."

Leah nodded wearily as her senses confirmed the wraithstone's destruction. She was watching for Rowen.

The sorcerer scrambled up from the ground where he'd taken cover. He waved at them.

Leah sighed with relief. She prodded her horse forward cautiously, and Fletcher followed. No sorcery blocked their way.

"Did you destroy the wraithstone completely?" asked Fletcher, dismounting next to Rowen.

"Your device blew it apart. Actually there were several spellstones linked together around the central wraithstone. Evidently the wraith took over the stones of the sorcerers it killed and used them to enhance its power. When I set up the device I noticed a broken spellstone and two others touching the wraithstone."

"So that was how the wraith got its enormous power," muttered Fletcher. "Let's take a look." He led the way into the marble pavilion.

"The broken stone may have been my father's," said

Leah. "Shaltus tried to plant the other pieces of it at Carlton. There must have been a large part left. Are you sure all the stones were destroyed?"

Rowen nodded. "Take a look for yourself. The explosion shattered the stones into a thousand pieces."

A life-sized statue of Shaltus lay on the floor of the gazebo. Its arms were broken. Its face was smashed— only the mocking smile remained.

Crystal shards of spellstones covered the ground and the blackened, cracked altar.

"I think it would be best if we destroy all the fragments," said Rowen. "They have no power now, but I'd rather be careful."

Numb with exhaustion, Leah watched silently as Fletcher transferred his spellstone back to Rowen in a short, intricate ritual of spells.

Then the sorcerer began to obliterate the tiny pieces of stone. One by one they vanished into fire and ash until none was left.

It was over.

Fifteen

The walls of the room were as familiar as an old glove, but now they seemed constricting and chafing, not comfortable or comforting. Since her father's death Leah had tried to think of them as her walls, her room, but they had never really been hers.

All that was truly hers now lay piled on her bed, bagged and packed and ready to go. There were clothes, toiletries, a bow and a quiver of arrows, a couple of books, a pearl necklace that her father had given her on her sixteenth birthday, a handful of coins saved over the years, cooking and camping gear, and a telescoping looking glass that she'd had since childhood.

She wondered if she should say good-bye before she left. But she really had no one to say good-bye to.

Since they'd returned to Castle Carlton she'd seen little of Rusty, Fletcher, or Michael Rowen. She'd assumed that they were busy negotiating with her half-brother to seal their bargain for a kingdom in exchange for destroying the wraith.

Barbara was being cared for by the Bishop Merion and several other N'Omb priests. They'd sent for some healers from the White Tower of N'Omb. The bishop seemed to think that they'd be able to erase most of the girl's horrifying memories and restore her sanity. They might have to wipe out some older memories as well and then reeducate her, but eventually she'd be almost normal.

The wedding would probably be postponed, but Leah guessed that within a year Barbara would be well enough to marry Michael Rowen.

Leah clenched her fists. She tried not to think about it. She didn't want to know why it was bothering her.

Perhaps that was why she didn't seek out Rowen and say good-bye. She didn't want to find out how painful that would be.

As for her half-brother, she'd composed a simple note telling him that she'd left—and would not return. When the servants arrived to help her with her baggage, she'd give one of them the note to take to Richard.

All during the long trip back to Castle Carlton from Bluefield Leah had tried not to think about the future. She'd joked with Rusty and Fletcher, chatted with Rowen, tended Barbara. She'd buried her feelings and fears beneath a mask of easy comradery. However, deep down she'd known all along that she would never be able to stay at Carlton, even if Richard accepted her return.

And he'd had to. When Michael Rowen described how she'd helped destroy the wraith, her half-brother had had no other choice. Yet his attitude was more of forgiveness than remorsefulness—as though she had done something wrong in spite of all the evidence to the contrary.

He'd condescended to let her remain at Carlton. But that was impossible. While she might be able to forgive Richard for ordering her execution, she would never be able to forget it.

When the news arrived that Geraed had taken over as chief of the Ayers tribe after receiving word of Quinen's death, Leah had thought about returning there. But she knew she could never really fit in as a Sylvan, even if they allowed a *shiffem* to stay.

She wondered if Geraed had exposed the Expansionist's plot. The message hadn't said. It had only told of Geraed's new position and of his offer to meet with Richard S'Carlton to discuss a new treaty. With Geraed as chief war between the Sylvan and the humans might be averted. However, Leah doubted that a lasting peace was possible—there was too much hatred.

The sound of someone knocking on her door interrupted Leah's thoughts. She opened the door and let in the servants. While they gathered her belongings together, she handed one of the women the letter she'd written to Richard. Then they carried her things down to the stable.

After they left she studied the room once more, searching for anything she might have missed.

The bare walls were cold and impersonal; yet in a way Leah hated to leave them. Carlton was the only security she had ever known, and now she was turning her back on it. She felt foolish and afraid, but she was too stubborn to change her mind.

She turned to leave and caught sight of herself in the mirror on her dresser. Her too-pale face stared back, impassively, locked in control, concealing the uncertainties and fear that made her tremble inwardly. Her moon-silver hair was plaited and bound around her head, human-style, and tucked neatly under a cap. She hated the rigidity of it, the tightness of the braids pulling at her scalp, the silly covering that really hid nothing.

She touched the cap gingerly. Suddenly she flung it off. She quickly untied the braids, pulled them down and unbound them. She took a comb from her trouser pocket and brushed out her hair until it hung loosely down to her waist. She thought of replaiting it into one braid in the comfortable Sylvan style. But she wasn't Sylvan any more than she was human. She was only herself, part of both, and perhaps that meant being neither.

As satisfied as she was ever going to be with her appearance she stuffed the comb back into her pocket and glanced around the room once more.

She felt lonelier than she had ever felt during a lifetime of loneliness. It was not just that she was leaving Carlton—and in spite of everything that was not easy—but rather it was that she'd grown used to Fletcher, Rusty, and Rowen's company. She fit in with them in a way that made her almost sorry she'd ever known them at all, for having known their friendship her loneliness was far harder to bear.

Struggling not to think about Rowen and the others, she headed for the stable.

The servants had left her gear in a heap near the stable door.

Leah surveyed the stock and chose two big geldings, one a bay, the other a brown. Although both belonged to her brother, she felt sure that he would not mind her taking them if it meant that she were leaving for good. She thought of using two of the Sylvan horses instead, but they were really overlarge even for her.

She saddled the bay and put a pack carrier on the brown. Then she began loading her belongings.

"Leah!"

She looked up to see Michael Rowen striding toward her. His left arm was still in a sling, but he'd drunk enough *tomaad* to ensure that it would heal rapidly.

"I was worried I wouldn't catch you. I just heard that you were leaving."

Afraid his deep gray eyes would see too much, she glanced away and busily continued packing.

"Yes."

"Where are you going?"

She studied the bay's mane without really seeing it. "I couldn't stay here. There's no place for me here anymore."

"You'll go to the Sylvan?"

She shook her head. "Even if my grandfather were still alive, I'm not sure I would fit in; without him I probably wouldn't even be welcome. I'm thinking of heading west, perhaps taking up your trade—selling my services as a sorceress."

"Rusty, Tim, and I have been talking and . . ."

The stable door banged open, interrupting Rowen. Fletcher slipped through the doorway. Rusty followed him. They were both laden with heavy armloads of baggage. They smiled at Leah before heading down the row of stalls to the new horses that Richard had given them as gifts.

"Where are you off to?" she asked with surprise. "Back to Bluefield so soon?"

"Bluefield? No." Rowen looked puzzled. Then he smiled. "Oh. I guess you haven't heard. We're leaving too, for good. Lord S'Carlton has withdrawn his offer of an alliance. He says your sister is hopelessly insane."

"What? But Bishop Merion thinks she'll be all right eventually."

"Richard S'Carlton knows that. He's just using it as an excuse. I don't think he ever intended to give me Bluefield. If Barbara weren't ill, he would have found another reason to break off the alliance—he doesn't want to give up that much valuable land now that he's got it. He paid us off in gold instead. Perhaps it's just as well." Rowen shrugged. "I was never completely comfortable with the idea of settling down in one place or sure I wanted the responsibility of running my own kingdom. And I never liked having to settle for a marriage of convenience."

Leah took a deep breath, raised her head, and met Rowen's eyes. "Then you didn't love Barbara?"

"No. I don't love Barbara."

Fletcher stepped out of the stall and walked toward them. "Have you asked her yet?" said the ex-priest.

"Asked me?"

Rowen nodded. "We want to make you an offer that we've been discussing. We were wondering if you'd be willing to ride along with us for a while. We can use another sorcerer in the group."

Stunned, Leah could only murmur, "I don't know."

Fletcher grinned. "How about it? We work well together."

Rusty came out of the stall leading one of the horses. He nodded agreement.

"I . . ." Leah looked back and forth unbelievingly at the three men. Their acceptance and sincerity were genuine.

The impassive mask she'd worn so long to conceal her feelings began to crack. She smiled hesitantly, then beamed and nodded, unable to speak.

Rusty's too-wise eyes seemed to twinkle at her. "You and Michael are going to make one hell of a team."

Rowen stepped forward, took her hand, and squeezed it gently. Then he lifted it to his lips and kissed it.

As Leah met his eyes she realized that all along they'd held a place for her that would be more of a true home than anything she'd ever had or ever dreamed of having.

COUSY BOOK